MEET THE RADISH

Also in this series

1: My Sister Sam
2: Meet the Radish

Look out for . . .

3: Here Comes Ellen
4: Secret Simon

Meet
the Radish

Jean Ure

Hodder
Children's
Books

a division of Hodder Headline plc

A Catalogue record for this book is available
from the British Library

ISBN 0 340 72722 5

Typeset by Avon Dataset Ltd, Bidford-on-Avon, Warks

Printed and bound in Great Britain by
Clays Ltd, St Ives plc

Hodder Children's Books
a division of Hodder Headline plc
338 Euston Road
London NW1 3BH

1

I can still remember the day the Radish came to live with us. I remember the day Mum told us about him.

'Abi,' she said, 'Sam! There's something I want to talk to you about.'

I remember me and Sam shooting these anxious glances at each other. Now what had we done? I thought Mum must have discovered the splodge of red paint on my bedroom carpet, even though I'd put a chair over it. Sam told me later that *she* thought Mum had come across the broken flower pots she'd hidden behind the compost heap. There's always something!

Mum must have seen our worried expressions.

'It's all right,' she said. 'It's nothing you've done – this time!'

Phew! What a relief. Our guilty secrets were safe! Sam looked at me and pulled a face. I pulled one back.

Sam and me are sisters – well, foster sisters, actually. But we are just as close as real sisters. Closer, sometimes. We never ever quarrel and we don't have secrets, either. Not from each other. Only from other people. Such as, for instance, Mum!

'Miss Davies rang this morning,' said Mum. 'There's this little chap she needs to place. Just for a while, until his mum gets herself sorted out. He's not too happy where he is at present.'

'No, some foster homes are really horrible,' said Sam.

Sam was in lots of different places before she came to us. She knows all about it.

'There's another boy there who bullies him,' said Mum. 'Miss Davies wanted to know whether we felt that we could take him. Of course I said yes! After all, we've got the room and one extra body won't make much difference. If we can have all these animals, I'm sure we can squeeze in just one little boy.'

I frowned. I wasn't sure I liked the way Mum had said 'all these animals'. As if we had too many of them. We've only got three! And they're only tiny.

There's Jack, who is mine, and Daisy, who is Sam's, and Felix, who is our cat. Jack is a terrier – a *small* terrier. Daisy is a bitsa, meaning bits of this and bits of that. She is bigger than Jack, but not by very much. And you can't really count Felix. I mean, cats don't take up any room at all, hardly.

I didn't want Mum suddenly deciding one of them had to go!

'*Three*,' I said to Mum, holding up three fingers. 'Just *three*.'

'Three animals, three children,' said Mum. 'I've spoken to your dad. He's quite agreeable.'

She didn't ask me and Sam if we were agreeable!

'What's his name?' said Sam.

Mum said his name was Gus. 'Gus Radeechy.'

That was how she pronounced it: Radeechy. It wasn't till we saw it written down that we discovered it was spelt R.a.d.i.c.e.

'Must be Italian for radish,' said Sam. She giggled. 'Gus Radish!'

So that was when we started calling him the Radish; before he even arrived.

'We'll have to get his room ready,' said Mum. 'We haven't got long, Miss Davies is bringing him round tomorrow afternoon.'

'*Tomorrow?*' I said. I thought we'd have at least a week to get used to the idea. We'd had to wait ages before they let Sam come to us.

Mum said that was different. We'd never fostered anyone before Sam and we'd had to be checked out.

'Don't we have to be checked out again?' I said. 'I mean, Sam is a *girl*.'

'Girl, boy, no difference,' said Mum.

Well! There is a great *deal* of difference, if

4

you ask me. But Mum said once you'd passed the test you didn't have to take it again.

'We're fit for fostering!'

'So we ought to be,' said Dad; and he winked. 'Foster by name, foster by nature!'

Dad makes that joke over and over. I suppose it's still quite funny. See, our surname is Foster. Anyway, Sam laughed. She hadn't heard it as often as me and Mum!

'Let's go and see to his bed,' urged Mum, and she led the way up the stairs with me and Sam following and Jack scampering ahead. He likes to be in on everything, does Jack. Felix would go nosing round later, in his own good time, and Daisy was in the garden on a mouse hunt. She spends hours hunting for mice. I sometimes think that's what she is: a mouse hound.

'What would a little boy like in his room?' wondered Mum. 'What can we put in here to make him feel welcome?'

She was really excited, you could tell. She

really liked the idea of having another child in the house. I began to suspect that maybe a boy was what she had secretly always wanted.

'We don't have any boy sort of things,' I said.

'Yes, we do!' Sam whirled round on me. 'We've got the family cars!'

The family cars are models that belong to my dolls' house. I know it is a bit childish to be still playing with dolls' houses when you are nearly eleven years old, but I have had my dolls' house since I was little. Dad made it for me. I like to redecorate it and rearrange the furniture and make new curtains from time to time. It is one of my *interests*. I didn't see why I should have to give away the family cars. How would the dolls' house people get around without them?

'They don't need them,' urged Sam.

'They do!' I said. 'The dad needs one for work and the mum needs the other for taking the children to school.'

'The children could walk to school! We walk to school.'

'Their school is too far away.'

'Why?' said Sam. 'Where is it?'

'Over the other side of town.'

'You're just making that up! You never even thought about it before!'

'I did, too!'

'You did not!'

'How do you know? You weren't here!'

'Girls, girls,' said Mum. 'Enough! We'll go into town tomorrow morning and pick up a few bits and pieces. Abi, go and get a clean sheet and pillowcase out of the airing cupboard.'

'They could go by *bus!*' hissed Sam, as I left the room.

I knew I was being mean. I'm not usually. It was just this sudden thought I'd had about Mum; about her secretly wanting a boy. Would she have liked *me* to be a boy? Had it been a bitter disappointment to her when I'd turned out not to be?

'Here's your baby, Mrs Foster! A dear little girl.'

'Oh,' says Mum, 'how lovely!' And all the time she's thinking to herself, 'Rats' tails and rubbish! I didn't want a rotten girl!'

Well, I didn't really suppose that's what she was thinking. But I just couldn't understand why she was so eager to have this Radish come and live with us.

'I thought you always wanted to be part of a large family?' said Mum, as I came back with the sheet and the pillowcase.

'That was when I was younger,' I mumbled.

Actually, as a matter of fact, it was when I was about six months younger. Before Sam came. When Mum first announced that we were going to be Foster by name and foster by nature, I'd had visions of the house being full to bursting point! Children everywhere. All shapes, all sizes. All different ages, boys and girls. I'd even planned how they could sleep in bunk beds around the walls. I really thought it would be fun.

But then Sam had come and now I wasn't sure that I wanted anyone else. Me and Sam were best mates! We went everywhere together, we did everything together. Mum sometimes complained it was like we were stuck with superglue. We didn't need any more kids in the house!

Specially not a *boy*.

'Boy's better than a girl,' said Sam.

I looked at her, doubtfully. 'You think so?'

'Yeah. Well. I mean—' Sam waved a hand. 'Girl might make things difficult.'

'How? How would she make things difficult?'

'Might try coming between us.'

'A boy could come between us!'

'Nah,' said Sam. 'A boy won't bother us.'

I still felt these little prickles of doubt. Sam herself is quite boyish. I mean, she's bigger than me, and stronger than me, and she likes doing boyish things such as kicking balls and climbing trees and even fighting. Suppose she and this Radish got all friendly together and started to hang out? They wouldn't want me trailing round after them. I'd be left on my own again! An only child, just like I always used to be.

He's only little,' said Sam, as if reading my thoughts.

That's what Mum had told us: just a little lad. But to Mum anyone under the age of about eighteen is little! I once even heard her referring to Sam as a *little lass*. For all we knew, this Radish could be the same age as we were.

And then Mum came bustling in, full of ideas about what we could buy to put in the spare bedroom to make it look more welcoming.

'I'll tell you what I'll do,' said Dad. 'I'll knock him up a toy box.'

'Sam didn't have a toy box,' I said.

'Sam was older,' said Mum. 'This little lad's only six.'

I relaxed a bit when Mum said that. I'd really been dreading that he might turn out to be some lumbering great hulk like the boys in our class at school. Big boys can be *such* a bore, pushing you around all the time and jeering at the games you play. 'Oh,' they go, 'that's a girl's thing!' As if girls' things aren't as good as boys'.

Six really *was* little. I couldn't see Sam hanging out with a six-year-old!

'He's had a bit of a rough start in life,' said Dad, 'from what we're told.'

'Oh?'

Sam looked up, quickly. She sounded sort of . . . defensive. I expect I would have sounded the same, in her place. 'Cos if anyone has had a rough start in life, it's Sam. First it was her mum dying when she was only little, which is just about the worst thing that can happen to a person. I think that if my mum died I wouldn't be able to go on living, except I suppose I would have to because of Jack. He loves me so! He would pine if I weren't here. So I would have to be brave, for his sake.

I know that Sam would have been brave as she is a very brave sort of person. But life is truly unfair! 'Cos shortly after her mum died her dad wasn't able to look after her any more, and ever since then she has had to live with her aunt and uncle and in various foster homes. Until, of course, she came to us, and now she is one of the family.

Anyway. I didn't reckon the Radish could have had anywhere near as terrible a time as Sam.

'What happened to him?' I said.

'Poor little mite!' Honestly, Mum had gone all marshmallowy. All soft and gooey. 'His step-dad was unkind to him and his mum really didn't look after him at all well. He's a very bruised little boy.'

Sam looked interested. 'You mean he's been bashed?'

'Well . . . let's just say that people haven't

been very nice to him. Even in his last foster home.'

'Why?' I said. 'What did they do to him?'

'Beat him?' said Sam.

'Starve him?' I said.

'They had these two big lads,' said Mum, 'who bullied him.'

You see? *Big* lads. Sam says I'm not being fair, she says girls can be bullies just the same as boys and I suppose she is right. But I was still glad that the Radish was only little!

I couldn't help wondering what Mum had meant when she said his step-dad was unkind to him. Had he bullied him as well? And his mum, not looking after him properly!

'That's rotten,' I said, 'having a mum that doesn't look after you.'

'At least he has a mum,' said Sam.

I didn't say any more after that as it is a subject Sam is rather sensitive about. But already I was beginning to feel a bit sorry for the poor little Radish, and a bit less mean and resentful.

Next morning, me and Mum and Sam caught the bus into town and went to Hamlyn's, the big department store in the Taberner Centre. There we picked a selection of toys to put in the Radish's toy box, which Dad had made out of an old tool chest.

'Just little things,' warned Mum. 'Nothing too expensive.'

It was really fun, choosing toys! I chose a painting book and some paints and a furry rabbit that he could cuddle in bed 'cos I thought he might be lonely, coming to a strange house. Sam chose a Turbo Ranger and a rubbery dinosaur. Mum got him a bat-and-ball game and a jigsaw puzzle and some Read Alone books.

'Suppose he can't read?' I said.

'Then you can read to him,' said Mum.

Me? Why me? Mum was the one who was so eager to have him! I was on holiday. We had three weeks to go before the Christmas term began, and me and Sam had things to do. We were going to make our own theatre! We'd worked it all out, how we were going to do it. We'd even drawn plans, with proper measurements. We'd aimed to get started this weekend – until Mum had gone and dropped the bombshell on us.

'I'll expect you two girls to lend a hand,' she'd said. 'You can't leave it all to your dad and me. We're one big family in this house.'

When we got home we put the toys in the toy box. It was a bit disappointing. They didn't even begin to fill it!

Mum said the Radish was bound to bring some things of his own, but I couldn't help remembering how Sam had turned up with almost nothing. It seemed really mean to give a poor little six-year-old a toy box with hardly any toys in it, so I sneaked into my bedroom and borrowed the family cars from the dolls' house garage. I could always put them back later, when he'd got bored with them. Or I could buy some more. And then I saw my old teddy bear that I'd had since I was about two, so I snatched him up as well. He was a bit worn at the edges, and one ear was chewed where Jack had got at it, but he looked nice and friendly.

When Sam saw what I'd done she wanted to put something in there as well, so she went rushing off to see what she could find. She came back with a special pen that had a view of St Paul's Cathedral in the top of it and a bright green squeaky toy in the shape of a hedgehog.

'That's Daisy's!' I said.

'I know,' said Sam. 'I told her she'd got to make a contribution.'

Dear Daisy! She is such a good little, meek little soul. If I'd nicked one of Jack's squeaky toys he would have given me all sorts of hassle. Jack is very protective of his toys.

So anyway, after that the toy box looked a little bit better. Now all we had to do was wait for Miss Davies to arrive. (Miss Davies is the lady from Social Services. She was the one who gave us the test to see if we were suitable for fostering. She is quite nice when you get to know her.)

'D'you remember the day she brought you?' I said to Sam. 'I gave Jack this huge big lecture before you came. I told him he'd got to be on his best behaviour. And the very first thing he did was to go and jump on you!'

'Yes, and that reminds me,' said Mum. 'You'd better keep him locked away when they get here. We don't want him frightening the little lad. He'll be nervous enough.'

'Mum!' I wailed. 'This is Jack's home!'

'It won't hurt him to stay in the kitchen for a while.'

I thought that was truly unfair. Just because Jack is a bit bouncy! Sam is bouncy, too; Mum didn't tell her to stay in the kitchen!

Actually, it's funny, that. Jack is bouncy and I am quiet – well, fairly quiet – while with Sam and Daisy it's the other way round. Daisy never bounces at anyone. She just sidles up to them, wagging her bum and making this little 'Whoo hoo!' noise like an old lady. It's her way of saying hallo.

Daisy was allowed to stay. So was Felix. Well, Felix just does his own thing. I'd thought of putting him in the kitchen with Jack, so's Jack wouldn't feel lonely, but when I tried to catch him, that wretched cat, he went rushing up the curtain and sat there on top of the curtain rail, all puffed up and smug. He gets away with a LOT, does Felix.

'Right,' said Mum. 'They'll be here any minute. Now, just remember, you two, he's a sad little scrap and I want you both to be nice to him.'

I was hurt. Of course we'd be nice! What did Mum think?

'No more Radish jokes,' said Mum.

Sam pulled a face. It's true, we had been making rather a lot of Radish jokes just recently.

'His name is *Gus*,' said Mum.

We nodded solemnly. His name was Gus.

And then there was a ring at the door, and Mum went out into the hall, and me and Sam stood waiting, trying not to look at each other for fear we might start giggling. I mean, there wasn't anything to giggle *about*; but when Sam repeated Mum's words to Daisy – 'Did you hear that, Daisy? His name is *Gus*' – I just nearly collapsed. I don't know why. There wasn't any reason.

We heard the front door opening, and we heard Mum's voice, and then we heard Miss Davies's voice, and then we heard Mum say, 'Come on in then, Gus! Come and meet the girls,' and this little procession trooped into the room.

Mum and Miss Davies and – Gus. His name was *Gus*. But it wasn't any use. Me and Sam caught each other's eye. Fatal! I clamped a hand to my mouth. Sam buried her face in Daisy's ruff. Little squeaks came out of us. The

Radish was wearing bright red cord jeans and a bright red puffa jacket. In addition, he had bright red hair that grew to a point on the top of his head. He looked exactly like –

A RADISH!

2

Mum looked at us, very annoyed. Miss Davies stared at us as if we were mad. She didn't know about the Radish jokes, so naturally she wouldn't have understood what we found so funny. But Mum understood and she went ballistic. It isn't very often Mum gets cross, but I could tell that on this occasion we'd seriously gone and blown it.

'Abi!' she snapped. 'Sam!'

The Radish just stood there, with his head hanging down and his thumb in his mouth, trying to hide behind Miss Davies. Of course we felt terrible. Well, I did, and I'm sure Sam did, too. He was such a sad, weedy little thing! It wasn't fair to laugh at him.

'This is *Gus*,' said Mum; and her eyes bored into us. 'Gus, this is Abi, and this is Sam.'

'And this is *Daisy*,' gushed Sam.

Daisy did her 'whoo hoo' noise and pranced across the room. She is so sweet when she does that! She bucks, like a little pony, and she has this big grin on her face. I just don't know how anyone could be scared of Daisy.

But guess what? The Radish gives this great scream and flings both his arms round Miss Davies's legs. And Mum practically spits blood.

'Sam!' she bellows.

'She won't hurt him,' said Sam. 'She just wants to be friendly.'

'She can be friendly some other time,' said Mum. 'Take her out to the kitchen with Jack.'

Well! I was glad Jack wasn't going to be the only one in exile any more but I hoped Mum didn't think he and Daisy were going to *live* in the kitchen. This was their home! And I still didn't see how anyone could be scared of a sweet little darling dog like Daisy.

'P'raps I ought to take Felix out there as well?' I suggested.

I could see Mum trying to decide whether I was being serious or whether I was being cheeky. I suppose to be honest it was a bit of both.

'Felix is no problem,' she said. She crouched down, next to the Radish. 'You're not frightened of our big white pussy cat, are you? He's over there, look! Can you see him?'

Very slowly, the Radish raised his head. Felix had by now come down from the curtain rail and was sitting on top of the television, washing himself.

'He's a very naughty cat, isn't he?' said Mum. 'Sitting on top of the television! What do you think he's doing there? Waiting for his favourite programme to start?'

The Radish put his thumb back in his mouth.

'Come and say hallo to him,' said Mum; and she led him across the room towards Felix. I waited for Felix, being Felix, to instantly get up and move. It's what he usually does if a

23

stranger tries to talk to him. If on the other hand a stranger doesn't *want* to talk to him, then Felix goes and purrs all round their legs and makes an absolute nuisance of himself.

'There!' said Mum. Give him a stroke . . . nice pussy!'

The Radish's hand wavered, uncertainly. Felix stopped in mid-lick. He gave the Radish one of his long, unblinking stares, very cool and considering. I waited for him to leap to the ground and go stalking off with his tail in the air, but would you believe it? He not only let the Radish stroke him, he even rolled over on to his back (almost falling off the television set) and let him tickle his tummy. That is something he never lets anyone do! Cats are just *so-o-o-o* contrary.

But I have to admit it was kind of sweet, the way the Radish's little beaky face lit up. You could tell he was ever so pleased that Felix had let him touch him. At least that was one of our animals that wouldn't have to go and live in the kitchen.

Miss Davies said that she couldn't stay, so Mum told me to look after the Radish while she went to see her out. I didn't know what she meant by look after him! What was I supposed to do? Sam came in just in time to rescue me.

'Don't tell me Felix is letting you *stroke* him?' she said.

The Radish looked up, beaming. He had this hole where his front teeth were supposed to be.

'Wow! That's an honour, that is,' said Sam. And then she said, 'Daisy would love it if you'd stroke *her*.'

'Maybe after tea,' said Mum, coming back into the room. 'Gus, why don't you go and take your clothes off while I get the kettle on? Abi will show you where.'

'Well, really! Mum had to go through the hall on her way to the kitchen. Why couldn't she take the Radish with her?

I knew why. It was because she wanted to *involve* me. But I wasn't sure I wanted to be involved! I didn't know anything about six-year-olds. It was ages since I'd been as young as that. How were you supposed to talk to them?

I cleared my throat.

'Come on, then,' I said. I held open the door and the Radish meekly trotted through. 'Down there.' I pointed to the row of pegs where we keep all our anoraks and stuff. 'OK?'

I suppose really I should have stayed with him. I don't know why I didn't. I think perhaps I was a bit nervous. I mean . . . he was so *weedy*. And I couldn't talk to him like Mum did! It embarrasses me to use baby talk.

I rushed back into the sitting room, where Sam was crooning over Felix. As soon as she saw me she swizzled a strand of hair on top of her head until it was standing up in a point.

'Stop it!' I said, trying not to giggle. I

snatched at Felix. 'Creep!' I told him. 'I s'pose now you think she'll give you prawns for supper?'

Felix gave me such a look! I'm not sure, but I could almost swear he winked at me . . . cats really are such slyboots!

Mum called to us from the kitchen: 'Tea's ready!'

'Goody,' said Sam. 'I'm starving!'

We bundled out into the hall, Sam in the lead. She stopped so suddenly that I went barging into her.

'What d'you do that for?'

Sam didn't say anything, but her mouth dropped open. I looked where she was looking. And my mouth dropped open. Standing by the row of pegs was the Radish. *Completely naked.* Mum had told him to go and take his clothes off, and that was what he had done.

They were all hanging there, on a peg. Red puffa jacket, red trousers, red jumper. Even his vest and underpants. Even his socks!

I swallowed. Sam turned and went belting down the hall.

'Muuuuuuum!' she yelled.

'What's the matter?'

'The R – I mean, Gus!' Sam pointed wildly. And at that moment Jack burst out of the kitchen and tore down the hall like a doggy express, straight for the Radish. The Radish screamed and I shrieked and Mum shouted, 'Abi, get that dog!'

She made it sound like it was my fault. But I wasn't the one who'd let him out! And anyway, he only wanted to say hallo.

After I'd collared him and Mum had cuddled the Radish and helped him put his clothes back on, we all went into the kitchen to have tea. Poor old Jack and Daisy were now shut upstairs in my bedroom.

'They can't be shut away *all* of the time,' I hissed at Mum; but she just shot me this really angry glare and so I thought, for the moment, I'd better keep quiet.

Later, when the Radish was sitting in front of the television watching some dotty little cartoon programme, Mum gave me and Sam this long lecture. She said, 'I'm really ashamed of you two girls! I expected better of you.'

She told us once again how the Radish was a poor little mite who'd been pushed about and ill-treated all his life long.

'He doesn't need you two poking fun at him!'

'We weren't poking fun,' said Sam.

'No?' said Mum. That's what it looked like to me!'

'We weren't laughing at *him*,' I said. 'Just—'

'Just what?' said Mum.

Sam put a finger in her hair and did her twizzling act. Before I could stop myself, a giggle had come shooting out of me.

'Right,' said Mum. 'That does it! If you're going to behave like this I shall have to tell Miss Davies we can't keep him. I shall tell her that you two girls are not mature enough to cope. Is that what you want me to do?'

Sam mumbled something. I looked down at the floor and scuffed at a hole in the lino.

'Well?' said Mum. 'Is it? Do you really want this poor little terrified scrap to be shunted off to yet another foster home? Before he's even had a chance?'

Slowly, still looking at the floor, I shook my head.

'Sam?'

'D'you think I could take Daisy in there and let her say hallo to him?' begged Sam.

Sam really loves Daisy. She loves her as much as I love Jack. It was my idea we should go to the rescue centre and adopt another dog that could be *Sam's* dog. So I was glad when Mum said she could introduce Daisy to the Radish 'so long as you do it gently, and don't force him', but I still felt upset about poor Jack being shut away.

'It's ever so unfair!'

'I can't help that,' said Mum. 'He's too

bouncy. Just give it a day or two.'

A *day or two*? A poor little dog that had never done anyone any harm, kept prisoner in his own house!

I flung down the cloth that I'd been using to wipe the dishes.

'If Jack's got to stay upstairs,' I shouted, 'I'll stay upstairs with him!'

'Suit yourself,' said Mum.

She'd really got the hump with me.

I arrived upstairs to find that Jack had scraped some of the paint off my bedroom door in his frenzy to get out. He was so indignant at being shut away! I didn't blame him, not one little bit.

'Don't worry,' I whispered. 'I still love you.'

Dad came home at six o'clock and Mum called me down for supper. I told Jack to be a good boy and that I would be back very soon, and I took him up a big Bonio to keep him happy. Sam told me that Daisy and the Radish were now friends.

'You like her now, don't you?' she said. The Radish nodded, and his little red top knot went pobble pobble. 'See, Daisy knows how to behave.'

Sam said it smugly. I felt like bashing her!

As soon as we'd finished supper Dad looked at Mum and said, 'Now?' and Mum said, 'Yes. Why not?' and Dad went racing off all boyish and eager to the garden shed to fetch the Radish's toy box that he'd made. Sam had wanted us to give it to him earlier but Mum had said no, we'd got to wait for Dad.

Dad was really excited. He'd tried ever so hard all through supper, telling the Radish some of his best jokes.

'Why did the gangster cut the legs off his bed?'

'*Because he wanted to lie low for a while!*'

'What did the dentist say in court?'

'*I swear to pull the tooth, the whole tooth and nothing but the tooth!*'

The Radish didn't even smile. I mean, I

know some of Dad's jokes are a bit corny, but I used to think they were hilarious when I was six years old. The Radish just sort of . . . *cringed*, every time Dad spoke to him. Yet my dad isn't at all a threatening sort of person! He's quite jolly and plump and just loves to make people laugh. I shouldn't think anyone in his life has ever been scared of Dad before. I felt kind of sorry for him.

Anyway, at least the toy box was a success. You should have seen the Radish's face when he was presented with it! His eyes went all round and owly and his mouth dropped into this great big O.

'There you are, lad.' Dad threw back the lid. 'All yours!'

The Radish shot a frightened look at Mum. It was like he *wanted* to believe Dad, but didn't quite dare.

'Yes, it's all right,' said Mum. It's for you . . . it's your toy box!'

The Radish just stood, with his hands

clasped beneath his chin, his eyes staring in wonderment at all the goodies we'd collected for him.

'This comes from me,' said Sam, taking out her special pen with the picture of St Paul's Cathedral. 'And this is from Daisy.' She pulled out the squeaky hedgehog. 'If you squeak it, she'll play with you.'

The Radish looked at Sam, wide-eyed.

'Well, go on!' she said. 'Squeak it!'

So he did, and Daisy immediately came scuttling over, with her 'whoo hoo hoo!' and very gently but firmly took it from him. The Radish gave a little gap-toothed gurgle of laughter.

'Look,' I said quickly, 'these are what I gave you!' I fished around for the family cars. 'And this – ' I seized on my old teddy bear – 'this is from Jack. It's a bit tatty but he really wanted you to have it. 'Cos he really wants to be friends with you,' I said. If only w—'

'Abi.' Mum put a finger to her lips.

'Don't push it, there's a good girl.'

Well! Just as I was starting to feel a bit calmer, and to think that fostering the poor little weedy Radish might be quite a good thing to do after all, Mum has to go and ruin it. It immediately made me feel disgruntled all over again. Why *couldn't* Jack say hallo? I'd hold him by the collar so that he couldn't jump up. I thought it was really mean of Mum and when supper was over I grumpily announced that I was going to spend the evening in my room.

'With Jack.'

I'd only been up there a few minutes when Dad knocked on the door. I thought he was probably feeling quite disgruntled too, because in spite of the toy box the Radish was still shrinking away from him.

'Ab?' he said. 'Want to take Jack for a walk?'

I jumped up. I love it when me and dad go for walks together.

'I'll get his lead!'

Of course Daisy had to come too. You can't take one of the dogs without the other; they always know. Sam stayed right where she was, sprawled on the floor with the Radish, helping him with his jigsaw puzzle, while Felix sat in a big purry heap nearby.

'Well!' Dad chuckled. 'Looks like they're getting on all right!'

I just grunted. Trying to smarm their way into Mum's good books was what they were doing. (I meant Felix and Sam.)

We walked the dogs up to the park.

'Don't fret yourself about Jack,' said Dad. 'It'll work out. Give the lad a chance. He's only just got here.'

'But he's even scared of you!' I said.

'He's had some bad experiences. It's going to take time.'

'He might at least have thanked you for the toy box,' I grumbled.

'He didn't have to thank me. Didn't you see

the expression on his face? Come on, lass!'
Dad ruffled my hair and I tried not to squirm.
I don't like it when people ruffle my hair! It is
rather *limp* sort of hair and it musses it up. But
I tried not mind 'cos at least Dad was
discussing things with me and not just being
humpish, like Mum.

'He's a right sorry little guy, isn't he? But
just think! If that was Jack who'd been badly
treated you'd do your best to make it up to
him, wouldn't you?'

'Ye-e-e-es,' I just stopped myself in time from
saying that Jack *was* being badly treated.

'You'd be the first to say he couldn't help
the way he was. You'd be falling over
backwards to make excuses for him! Poor little
dog, you'd be saying. It's not his fault! He can't
help it.'

I knew that Dad was right.

'I'll try to think of him as a dog,' I assured
Dad, solemnly.

'Well . . . I didn't quite mean that,' said Dad.

'But if you think it will help—'

'It will,' I promised.

It didn't stop me saying pointedly to Sam when we got back that I had taken *her dog* for a walk.

'I'd have come, if you'd asked me,' said Sam. 'I didn't know you wanted me.'

'Well, anyway,' I said. 'Where's Mum?'

'Upstairs with the Radish. Tucking him in.'

'Oh, good!' I said. 'That means Jack can stay down.'

'He kissed me goodnight,' said Sam.

'Really,' I said. I said it sort of . . . offhandedly, just to show that I wasn't impressed.

'And Daisy.'

'And Felix too, I suppose!'

'Felix has gone with him.'

I said, '*Felix?*'

'He carried him up there.'

'Felix let him?' That cat is so two-faced!

'D'you remember when you first came?' I said. 'You tried to get him to sleep with you and he wouldn't?'

'Well.' Sam shrugged. 'He's littler than I am.'

'All the same,' I said.

I was in a really bad mood. I just couldn't help it. I felt cross with Sam and cross with Mum and even cross with Felix. The one person I was trying very hard *not* to be cross with was the Radish. I kept reminding myself that he hadn't asked to come here. He hadn't even asked to be born.

I made up my mind that tomorrow I would make a determined effort to be kinder to him.

3

It wasn't easy, being kind to the Radish. I mean, not that I was *un*kind. I tried really hard to make him feel at home. But he was just so . . . *cringy*. Talk about not saying boo to a goose! The poor little weedy Radish wouldn't have said boo to an *ant*.

I had to keep reminding myself that it wasn't his fault. He couldn't help being the way he was. I did what I'd promised Dad I would do: I pretended he was a dog! I know that sounds really stupid, but it is just *so* difficult when you make this huge special effort to be nice to someone and all they do is shrink away like they think you're going to bash them.

What I did, I imagined how it would be if Jack had been badly treated and ended up as a pathetic quivering heap, hiding away in corners and shaking every time anyone went near him.

It nearly broke my heart when I imagined it happening to Jack!

I did my best to feel the same about the Radish. Whenever I felt mean thoughts coming over me, such as 'This is going to ruin all the rest of the holidays!' or 'I wish Miss Davies had never brought him!' I turned the Radish into a sad little dog rescued from a doggy hell.

It was easier for Sam 'cos she had Daisy. Poor Jack was still in exile. Also, Sam is very bright and bubbly and doesn't seem to notice if people cringe away from her. She just carries on the same as usual. If I think someone doesn't like me I get really put off. I sort of . . . clam up, and can't think of anything to say. Dad, on the other hand, can always think of things to say. He can always find a joke to crack or a funny remark to make. Or else he puts on all these silly voices and gets you laughing. But even Dad couldn't raise a smile from the Radish.

Mum was the only one he really seemed happy with. He followed her round like a little lost thing, always clinging to her skirts or hiding behind her legs.

'How long is he going to be here?' I asked Mum, on Saturday evening.

Mum pursed her lips. 'As long as it takes.'

She was still a bit umpty with me.

'As long as it takes to *what*?' I said.

'As long as it takes his mum to get herself sorted and provide some kind of a home for him. Until she does, he stays here with us.'

'I was only asking,' I said.

'Yes,' agreed Mum. 'But why were you asking?'

'Because Jack can't stay in exile for ever!' I cried.

'Oh, Abi!' Mum suddenly relented. She put an arm round me and gave me one of her old mumsy-type cuddles. 'I'm sorry! I know this isn't easy for you.'

'It's not easy for Jack,' I mumbled.

'No, it isn't, but it won't last for ever. Give the poor little soul a chance!'

That's what Dad had said. But I'd given him a chance! I'd spent the whole day being as nice as nice could be.

'I'll tell you what,' said Mum. 'Tomorrow morning we'll all go for a walk together. We'll get in the car and go over to Happy Valley. If Jack's out in the open he won't jump up. It might be a way of letting them get to know each other. Shall we do that? Yes?'

'Yes!' I nodded, and felt quite cheered up.

And then Mum added, 'At least it'll get the wind out of his tail. A good long walk and he'll be so tired he'll be only too happy to stay in your room and sleep.'

Needless to say I immediately felt plunged into deepest gloom all over again.

'He doesn't want to stay in my room!' I wailed. 'He wants to be downstairs with the rest of us!'

'Let's give it a go and see what happens,' said Mum.

Well! You'll never believe it, but Mum's plan worked. To begin with, the Radish held on tight to Mum's hand and scuttled for safety behind her legs every time Jack came anywhere near. But then me and Sam started throwing sticks, and Jack and Daisy got hold of one between them and did their big bold stick act, tug-tug-tugging with their bums stuck up in the air, looking really comical, and the Radish gave this funny little gurgling laugh he does, showing the gap in his teeth, and Mum said, 'They're funny, aren't they? They're playing tug of war!'

After a bit Daisy lost interest and went scampering off to look down some holes she'd found, but Jack is a real stick dog. He never gives up! He'll run and chase all day long.

'Do you want to throw one for him?' said Mum.

Next thing we know the Radish is picking

up all these weedy little twigs and lobbing them into the air, and Jack's leaping up and catching them, and the Radish is gurgling fit to bust with his little red top knot pobbling like mad, and it's a real victory!

On the way there, Mum had driven the car with the Radish sitting next to her, and me and Sam and Dad all squashed up at the back with the dogs. On the way home, Dad sat in front and the Radish sat between me and Sam with the dogs on our laps. Jack kept blobbing at him with his tongue, 'cos he's a bit of a licker, is Jack. Every time he blobbed, the Radish squealed and crimped his hands into little fists and beat at his cheeks with them. It alarmed me at first. I thought Mum was going to start shrieking, 'Abi, control that dog!' But I needn't have worried. I have since discovered that it's what the Radish does when he's happy: he crimps his fists and beats his cheeks and squeals! He's got some really funny little habits. You just have to get to know them.

Mum obviously recognised it as a happy squeal and not a frightened one 'cos she didn't say a word, just calmly went on driving and having this conversation with Dad. When we got home she said to me, 'There! I told you it would work out.'

The rest of the day was really good. Sam and me taught the Radish how to play Snap – imagine! He'd never played it before – then I dug out some of my old board games that I still had, like Snakes & Ladders and the Magic Castle, and we played at those till teatime. The Radish was almost starting to behave like a normal six-year-old! Well, not that I can properly remember being six, it is such a long time ago. But he was doing lots of gurgling and cheek-pummelling and wasn't shrinking away any more, except from poor Dad. I felt so sorry for Dad! It is horrid not to be liked and Dad hadn't done a thing to deserve it.

'I bet some man's been horrible to him,' said Sam.

'His step-dad,' I said.

'I bet he belted him.'

'Dad wouldn't ever do a thing like that!'

'Yeah, but he's not to know,' said Sam. 'He probably thinks all men are like it.'

In some ways Sam is quite wise. I expect it is all the experience she has had. Experience of life, I mean. I have just lived quite safe and cosy with my mum and dad. I suppose I have been very lucky.

On Monday afternoon Miss Davies called round. It was just a routine visit, the same as she'd done with Sam when Sam first came, but the Radish went all white and wobbly and started trembling. I couldn't think what the problem was. It's true Miss Davies is not what you would call a fun person, meaning she doesn't laugh very often or make jokes, but she isn't sinister or frightening. In fact, under the stern exterior she is quite kind. Sam said what it was, most probably, the Radish was scared she'd come to take him away.

'They do that, sometimes.'

'What, without asking you?'

'They don't *ask* you. They just say you've got to leave and go somewhere else. Like if people don't want you any more.'

I thought that was terrible! To know that back on Friday Mum could have rung Miss Davies to say that me and Sam weren't mature enough to cope and Miss Davies could have come and taken the Radish away and it wouldn't have mattered one bit what *he* wanted. His little feelings wouldn't have come into it.

But anyway Miss Davies hadn't come to take him anywhere, she simply wanted to make sure he was getting on all right. After she had gone we all breathed a sigh of relief.

'See?' said Sam. 'Nothing to worry about! No one's going to take you anywhere. Let's go and watch some telly!'

We all trooped into the sitting room and sat down in a row on the sofa. The dogs came with us. Me and Sam had been working on our theatre and didn't really want to watch television, but we just felt that perhaps we ought to keep the Radish company. His thumb had gone back into his mouth and he was sucking away like it was a lollipop. It's always a bad sign when the Radish sucks his thumb.

Quite suddenly, I had an idea.

'Let's hold hands,' I said. 'All hold hands!'

'Hold *hands*?' said Sam.

'Yes! All hold hands!'

And then she got the message.

'Yeah, right! Let's hold hands!'

We turned it into a game. The dogs played as well, so that in the end the Radish forgot about his thumb and about Miss Davies coming to take him away. He was kicking and squealing and pummelling his cheeks like mad. It's ever such a good feeling when you can make a little boy like that happy!

I went to bed that night with this warm glow of satisfaction. Miss Davies had been and gone, Jack was no longer in exile, and for the first time since the Radish had come to us I truly believed that things would work out.

But oh! Disaster! Next morning, when me and Sam were in the garden showing the Radish how Jack could play football, Mum came out looking a bit annoyed and said, 'Some dog has gone into Gus's room and piddled on the rug.'

'It's not Jack!' I said.

'Well, it can't be Daisy,' said Sam.

'It has to be one of them,' said Mum.

'I *know* it's not Daisy,' said Sam, ''cos I had my bedroom door closed all night.'

'Abi? Did you have your door closed?'

'Yes, I did!' I said.

'But Daisy has been downstairs with me all the time,' said Sam.

'So's Jack!' I said.

'What about when you went to the bathroom?' demanded Mum.

'Daisy came with me!' Sam said it

triumphantly. She wasn't having *her* dog blamed.

'What's she want to do that for?' I said.

'She likes to roll on the flannel.'

'Ugh!' I said. 'That's disgusting!'

'No it's not! She thinks she's washing herself. Anyway, it's my flannel.'

'Abi?' said Mum. 'Where was Jack?'

I hesitated. I could hardly say that he liked to roll on the flannel too; not after telling Sam it was disgusting. (I didn't really think it was disgusting. I thought it was quite sweet. I just didn't want Jack getting the blame.)

'Did you leave your bedroom door open?'

'Um—' I was tempted to lie and say no. But I'd left it too late!

'If he's going to start behaving like that,' said Mum, 'he'll have to stay downstairs at night.'

'Mum!' I looked at her, hurt. How could she suggest such a thing? Jack has slept with me since he was a tiny pup. 'He's never done anything like that before,' I pleaded.

'It's probably a touch of jealousy,' said Mum.

'*Jealousy*? You mean . . . he's jealous of the Radish?'

'Abi, how many more times?' snapped Mum.

'Sorry, sorry! I mean Gus.'

'It's possible. Dogs can get jealous.'

'He wasn't jealous when Sam came!'

'No, well, that was a bit different. He didn't have to be shut away from Sam.'

'So it's not his fault!' I cried. 'And it's not fair to punish him!'

'I'm not punishing him. I simply said, if it happens again—'

'Oh, stop it!' yelled Sam. 'You're frightening the Radish!'

Mum didn't snap at Sam like she'd snapped at me. Instead, she swooped on the Radish and started crooning over him.

'It's all right, pet, it's all right. No one's cross with you. You weren't to blame! It was that naughty Jack, sneaking into your room.'

The poor old Radish was shaking like a leaf. He was shaking so much his top knot was pobbling.

'Jack's the one that ought to be told off,' said Sam. 'He's such a *bad* boy!'

Mum said firmly that no one was being told off.

'But I don't want a repetition! In future, Abi, you make sure he stays with you in the morning. Either that, or keep your bedroom door shut.'

I meant to. I really really meant to! But I'm not used to shutting him in. I went off to the bathroom as usual and just clean forgot about it. Next thing I know, Mum's yelling up the stairs: 'Abi! Have you let that dog out?'

I flew back along the passage. 'No! I've only just opened the door!'

'You'd better be right,' said Mum; and she comes charging up the stairs and heads straight for the Radish's room.

'*Abi!*' she thunders.

My heart went clunking right down into my shoes.

'What is this?' demanded Mum.

There was a horrid wet patch in the middle of the rug . . .

'Mum,' I begged, 'he wouldn't! I know he wouldn't! He just wouldn't do a thing like that!'

'But he has,' said Mum. 'And in exactly the same place as before! I'm sorry, Abi, but from now on he's going to have to stay downstairs.'

'Oh Mum, no, please!' I said. '*Please*, Mum! He'll be so unhappy! Give him one more chance, I beg of you!'

I put my hands together and made like I was praying, but Mum wouldn't budge.

'We can't afford to have the place ruined. Other dogs sleep in the kitchen; there's no reason why he shouldn't.'

'Well, if he's got to, Daisy ought as well!' I said. 'You can't make him sleep by himself. He'd be lonely!'

Mum agreed to this. She said it was something that should have happened a long time ago. She said it was ridiculous, our sheets constantly being covered in dogs' hairs, and even sometimes muddy pawprints, and that from now on they could stay together in a dog bed in the kitchen.

'They haven't *got* a dog bed!' roared Sam.

'We'll get them one,' said Mum. 'They don't need one just at this moment.'

'What about me?' Sam looked at Mum, all truculent. 'You got me a dog so's I'd have something to cuddle.'

'We got you a dog,' said Mum, 'to help you settle down. You *have* settled down.'

'But I might get unsettled!'

'I don't think so,' said Mum.

Sam was really upset about Daisy being banished to the kitchen. I said that I was upset too, and that it was worse for me because I had *always* slept with Jack, but Sam pointed out that if I'd only remembered to keep my door shut it wouldn't have happened. She said it was all my fault and it wasn't fair that Daisy had to stay downstairs just because of Jack piddling on the Radish's rug.

We had our very first quarrel and I hated it.

It took me forever to get to sleep that night. Poor Jack barked and barked. I could hear him scratching at the kitchen door and I even went into Mum and Dad's room and pleaded with Mum to let him come upstairs, but she was so hard-hearted!

'Just ignore him,' she said. 'He'll get used to it.'

He stopped barking in the end and I suppose I must have fallen asleep because if I hadn't fallen asleep I wouldn't have been able to wake up again, which I did at quarter to six, an hour that is practically *unheard of*. For me to wake up, I mean.

My immediate thought was for Jack. Could I hear him crying? I could! I was sure I could! I made up my mind that I would go downstairs and curl up with him on the kitchen floor so that Mum would find me there when she came to get breakfast. I would pretend I had been there all night and she would immediately feel guilty and say she was sorry for being so mean. She would promise me that tomorrow the dogs could come back upstairs again and sleep with us.

I crept out of bed, tiptoed across the room, opened my door just the tiniest crack and oozed out into the passage.

I couldn't hear any sounds from the kitchen, but there was a light coming from the Radish's room, and strange swooshing sounds. Swoosh, swoosh! Swoosh, swoosh! What on earth was he up to?

'Hey, Radish!' I whispered. 'What's going on?'

I pushed open the door and peered round. The Radish started, guiltily. He was kneeling on the floor, with a tooth mug full of water, scrubbing at something with the bathroom nailbrush.

'Whatever are you doing?' I cried.

4

I suppose I would have had to tell Mum sooner or later, even though it would have felt like snitching. I mean, for one thing I couldn't let her go on thinking it was poor Jack that was guilty. That wouldn't have been fair to Jack! But anyway, as it happened, I didn't have to tell her 'cos Mum was already awake and on her way to investigate.

We talked about it later, just her and me.

'I've heard about wetting the bed,' I said. But wetting the *rug?*

And then Mum told me what the poor little boy had been doing. He'd been so terrified of messing up the sheet that he'd taken his pillow and his duvet and gone to sleep on the rug every night. He'd hoped, if he'd had an accident, he'd be able to scrub it clean before anyone discovered.

'That is just so *sad*!' I said.

'It is sad,' agreed Mum. 'But he's rather a sad little fellow.'

'Did he think you'd be cross with him?'

'He thought I'd punish him.'

'Punish him? For something he can't help?' How could anyone be so cruel? To a little six-year-old boy!

'It's the way he's been treated,' said Mum.

'But it's like people hitting dogs for making puddles in the wrong places!'

'Yes.' Mum pulled a face. 'I'm sorry about poor Jack getting the blame! But at least I didn't hit him.'

'You just made him sleep in the kitchen,' I muttered.

'The kitchen is the place for a dog to sleep,' said Mum. And then, before I could start arguing – which I was going to, you just bet! – she quickly added, 'I hope you didn't make little Gus feel too guilty?'

'I didn't mean to,' I said. 'I just asked him

what he was doing. I mean, I was like . . . really surprised!'

'Maybe you should go and have a word with him.'

'Me?' I wasn't sure I liked that idea. 'What would I say to him?'

'Just be nice. Reassure him! Tell him you're not cross.'

I wrinkled my nose. 'Why should he think I'd be cross?'

'Because of Jack. He feels it's his fault Jack's not allowed to sleep upstairs any more.'

'Mum, *can't* he?' I begged. 'It's so unfair!'

'We'll see,' said Mum. 'You go and comfort Gus and maybe I'll think about it.'

The Radish was in the garden. He was squatting at the edge of a flowerbed, earnestly poking at the earth with a bit of twig. He looked like a garden gnome, with his funny little pobbly top knot. I instantly imagined a whole cluster of garden gnomes, all with pobbly top knots, and had to fight back a giggle. It wasn't funny!

'Hi,' I said, and the Radish nearly topped over into the flowerbed. He always jumped when anyone spoke to him.

'What are you up to?' I crouched down next to him. 'Are you looking for something?'

'Looking f'wormth,' whispered the Radish.

'Looking for worms? That sounds interesting,' I said. 'Have you found any yet?'

Slowly, the Radish shook his head. I took his tiny bit of twig and poked around with it in the earth. Unfortunately I poked too vigorously and the twig went and snapped.

'Bother!' I said. 'Now look what I've done! I've gone and broken your twig.'

The Radish bit his lip.

'I'll get another one,' I said. I marched over to the privet hedge and tore off a couple of bits of privet. 'There you are!' I handed one to the Radish. 'Now we can both look for worms.'

We squatted there together poking with our bits of privet in the flowerbed.

'Funny,' I said, 'you'd think there'd be hundreds, wouldn't you? They must have gone down really deep. Maybe that's what they do in dry weather . . . go down deep in search of water. D'you reckon?'

'Mm.' The Radish nodded.

'So what are you going to do with these worms when we find them?' I said.

'Keep ath pet-th.'

'Keep as pets?'

'Get a bockth an' put 'em in.'

Well! I didn't want to say anything to discourage him – I mean, we were *almost* having a normal conversation – but I do happen to be something of an animal lover. I am against all forms of cruelty to living creatures; even worms. So as gently as I could I said, 'I'm not sure that worms would like being kept in a box.'

'Bokth wiv *erf*,' the Radish assured me.

'Oh! Right. Well, a box with earth would be better than a box without earth. But I don't think Mum would let you have them in your bedroom. And they wouldn't be all that much fun,' I said. 'I mean, you couldn't cuddle them or take them for walks, could you?'

The Radish looked at me doubtfully.

'Imagine!' I said. I picked up a non-existent worm and made like I was cuddling it. 'Ugh! It's all slippy and slimy! Watch out, it's escaping! Get it back, quickly, before it disappears!'

The Radish watched in silent wonderment as I sprang to my feet and chased the worm round the garden.

'Gotcha!' I pounced. 'If you feel that frisky, my boy, you'd better come for a walk and get the wind out of your tail. Let me put you on your lead.' I bent down and clipped an imaginary lead to an imaginary collar. 'Come along, wormie! Walkies!'

Very solemnly, me and my worm trailed up the garden path and back round in a circle to the flowerbed. And oh, brilliant! I'd got the Radish giggling.

'You want a go?' I said. 'Here!'

I handed him the imaginary lead. The Radish took it and went stomping off across the grass.

'Careful!' I warned. 'Don't drag him! He's only a little worm!'

We had a lot of fun with that worm.

'We'll call him Wilfred,' I said, 'and he'll be our secret . . . just between you and me. So if I suddenly say to you, "Where's Wilfred?" you've got to make something up, like "He's in my pocket" or "He's sliming about the floor" and everyone'll go "Who's Wilfred? What are you talking about?" and we'll just look at each other like *this* – ' I closed one eye in a wink – 'and won't tell them. Right?'

'Wight.' The Radish pobbled his top knot and blinked rapidly with both eyes. 'Won't tell!'

'By the way,' I said, as we sat on one of the low branches of the apple tree, swinging our legs, 'I thought you'd like to know that Jack's probably going to come back upstairs again and he's asked me to say that he's not in the least bit cross with you 'cos he's not a dog that bears grudges, and when he comes back upstairs he's going to go into your bedroom and jump on top of you while you're in bed and *lick you to pieces!*'

And I went blob-blob-blob with my tongue, pretending to be Jack, and the Radish squealed and pummelled his cheeks so I knew that he was enjoying it.

'Another thing,' I said. 'You know how me and Sam call you the Radish? Well, I just wanted to say that we don't do it 'cos we're laughing at you, we do it 'cos it's a *nickname*. And you only give people *nicknames* if you like them. A *lot*. So when we call you the Radish it means we like you and think that you're special. Isn't that right?' I said, as Sam and the dogs came bounding down the garden. 'The Radish is *special*.'

'Absolutely,' said Sam. And then, all

suspicious, she goes, 'What have you two been talking about all by yourselves?'

The Radish flickers this anxious glance at me.

'Worms,' I say.

'Worms?' says Sam.

'Wormth,' says the Radish. And we look at each other and wink. Well, I wink. The Radish can't quite manage it. He just screws up his eyes.

In the end, later on, I had to tell Sam. I mean about the Radish going to sleep on the floor. It wasn't snitching. It's just that we have sworn this oath not to have secrets from each other. And I knew she'd never let on to the Radish.

'Sleeping on the *floor*?' said Sam. 'Poor little—'

I can't write the word she said! It's one we're not supposed to use.

'It's all right now,' I assured her. 'Mum's told him there's nothing to worry about. It doesn't matter if he does have an accident. Nobody's going to get mad at him.'

I was glad I'd let Sam into the secret. It meant we were friends again. Not that we'd ever really stopped being but I'd hated it when we'd quarrelled. The only thing I didn't tell her about was Wilfred the Worm. That was between me and the Radish!

When it came to bedtime, I mean me and Sam's bedtime, I looked very hard at Mum and said, 'I did what you told me. I talked to the Radish.'

'Gus,' said Sam, kicking at me. I knew she thought I'd gone and blown it.

'The Radish,' I said. 'It's OK, Mum, I've explained to him, it's a *nick*name. And he *likes* it. 'Cos it means he's special. So please can Jack and Daisy come back upstairs again?'

Mum hummed and hahed and whiffled on for a bit about dirty sheets and muddy pawprints, but then darling Dad spoke up and said he didn't think he could take another night of Jack barking and carrying on, and so at last Mum gave way and merely contented herself with a little lecture about 'not letting them up there with dirty feet'.

'As if we *would*,' said Sam.

'We *wouldn't*,' I said.

'Oh, get away with you!' said Mum. 'You're not the ones that have to wash the sheets.'

Me and Jack snuggled down beneath the duvet and I was so happy to have him back that I fell asleep almost at once and slept right round till morning. Well, almost morning. It was quarter to five when Jack woke me up, and I don't call *that* morning. I call that an ungodly hour. (That is what Dad calls it, specially in the depths of winter, when he's dragged out of bed to go and do an emergency job on someone's burst pipes.)

'Wossamadder?' I mumbled. Jack had suddenly sprung off the bed and shot across to the door. I thought he wanted to go down to the garden, which is *such* a drag but you have to take him. I was just about to slither out from under the duvet when the door opened and a little ghost-like shape drifted across the room. It was the Radish!

'Radish,' I said, 'what's wrong?'

He was standing by the side of my bed, sucking his thumb. In one hand he held his furry rabbit that we'd bought him.

'What is it? Have you had a nightmare?'

He shook his head.

'So what's the matter?'

With his thumb still in his mouth he mumbled, 'I done it again.'

'You've *done* it again?'

And then I suddenly realised what he was talking about.

'Oh, Radish!' I scrambled into a sitting position. 'Mum told you, it doesn't matter! Don't worry!'

His little face was all white and puckered. I could just make it out by the light that came through my bedroom curtains. He whispered something that sounded like 'Buddatheedollwed.' It took me a second or so to work it out: 'But the sheet's all wet.'

'Well, then,' I said brightly, 'we'll go and put it in the washing machine. *And* your pyjamas. We can get them washed and dried before anyone's even up!'

Me and Jack and the Radish all padded out of my room and into the Radish's. I stripped off the sheet and got him out some new pyjama bottoms, then we stole downstairs as quiet as could be, closed the kitchen door so's no one would hear us, and shoved everything into the machine.

'What I'll do,' I said, 'I'll put it on short wash.'

Mum would have been dead surprised to learn that I understood about the washing machine! She always says that if only me and Sam knew the amount of work we caused we'd take a bit more trouble to try and stay clean. But honestly, there's nothing to it! I don't know why Mum makes such a fuss. The machine does all the work. Well, apart from the ironing, but ironing isn't work. I don't think it is. I think ironing is *fun*. I quite often do a bit of ironing, especially the straight things. They're the most fun.

I can't imagine what Mum's problem is!

While the sheet and the pyjamas were being swooshed and spun we took Jack into the garden. It was warm out there, and quite light.

'Imagine! We might see a fox,' I said.

But the Radish was sucking his thumb. And he had gone all trembly. I knew it wasn't because he was cold. It was because he was frightened.

'There's nothing to be scared about,' I said. 'Everybody wets the bed occasionally. I used to wet my bed all the time, practically, when I was little.'

Actually it was when I was four years old and came out of hospital after having my tonsils out. And then I only did it for a month or two. But I thought it might cheer the Radish up to feel he wasn't the only one.

'How old woth you?' he said.

'Oh, about . . .'

The Radish looked at me trustingly.

'About your age,' I said.

I'd hoped it would comfort him, but he still seemed bothered. He tucked his hand into mine as we went back indoors.

'Did they make you wear the label?'

I said, 'What label?'

'Wounda neck.'

Label round the neck? What was he talking about?

'No one's going to make you wear any labels,' I said. 'Why should anyone want to make you wear a label?'

Later that day I asked Mum what he could have meant. (She knew we'd washed the sheet, by the way. She'd heard the machine going. But sometimes Mum can be really tactful. She'd crept downstairs, seen what was happening and gone straight back up again. Good old Mum!)

'He seemed to be worried we were going to make him wear a label,' I said.

Mum was as puzzled as I was. She said she would ask Miss Davies, and later on she told me about it.

'It was his step-dad. He used to hang this label round his neck saying *I WET THE BED*. He used to make him stand outside in the street wearing it.'

'*Mum!*' I stared at her in horror. I just couldn't believe anyone would do such a thing.

'I'm afraid some people are very cruel,' said Mum.

When I told Sam about it she was so indignant. She said, 'What about his mum? Why didn't she stand up for him?'

'I don't know,' I said. 'Maybe she was too scared.'

'She can't have been much of a mum!' cried Sam.

In the afternoon we took the dogs up to the park and the Radish came with us. He wanted to walk between us and hold on to our hands, so we let him even though it meant we couldn't run and play sticks the same as we usually did. But then Jack made off with another dog's ball and I had to go chasing after him to rescue it, and when I got back I heard Sam saying, 'See, poor Daisy was *really* ill-treated. She lived with this man and this woman and the man used to shove her around and she was so scared of him she started to piddle herself whenever he came near, and d'you know what he did? He used to rub a bit of cloth in it and tie it round her neck and make her stand outside in the street, even if it was freezing cold or pouring with rain, poor little Daisy.'

I listened in growing amazement. I knew for a fact, 'cos they'd told us at the rescue centre, that Daisy's owner had been a sweet old lady who had died!

But the Radish's eyes had gone all owly. His

thumb stole up to his mouth.

'What 'bout Jack?' he whispered.

'Poor Jack,' said Sam. 'He was ill-treated too. Wasn't he?'

She turned to me and screwed her face into a hideous gargoyle expression. I knew she was signalling me to agree with her. I nodded meekly.

'He was beaten and kicked by this horrible man.'

'Thame man?'

'No! This was a different man. He was vicious and cruel. So for a long time Jack thought all men were like that. He was really scared. Wasn't he?'

I nodded again.

'He was even scared of Dad! And Dad's the biggest softie in the world. He wouldn't hurt a fly.'

'No, he wouldn't,' I said. At least that bit was true!

'But they're all right now, him and Daisy.

They're happy now. Everyone's happy that lives in our house. 'Cos nobody beats you or ties things round your neck or makes you stand in the rain. Not in our house.'

'Jack 'n Daithy lock inna kitchen,' whispered the Radish.

'Oh, yeah, well! That was just 'cos Mum gets a bit umpty about muddy paw marks on the sheets. Anyone's mum'd get umpty about muddy paw marks.'

I saw a doubt creep into the Radish's eye.

'She doesn't really mind,' I said hastily, before Sam could undo all her good work. 'She thinks it's quite funny, actually.'

'That's right,' said Sam. 'She laughs about it. Look at those muddy pawprints, she goes, laughing away.'

'Muddy pawprints, tee hee,' I chortled. And then I thought that perhaps we were overdoing it slightly. 'Let's go home,' I said, 'and play a game. What game would you like to play?'

'Nap!' said the Radish.

Snap. Me and Sam exchanged glances. Snap is such a childish game! But we were the ones that had taught it to him, so I guess we only had ourselves to blame.

'Snap snap snap!' cried Sam. 'Let's you and me race Abi to the gate!'

5

Now that the Radish wasn't so shy any more, he was quite fun. Well, for a six-year-old! Him and me got this thing going about Wilfred the Worm. Like sometimes we'd be sitting watching telly and I'd say, 'Want to cuddle Wilfred?' and I'd make this big production of letting an imaginary worm go slithering through my hands and into the Radish's, and the Radish would sit there beaming away with his gap-toothed beam and cradling Wilfred in his arms like a baby. Sometimes we even cooed over him! Sam just stared at us as if we were mad, but she never asked us what we thought we were doing. I think she was scared we wouldn't tell her, and she was right! This was between me and the Radish.

Then one day at dinner the Radish got really bold. He leaned across the table and whispered, 'Abi, Wiffwid 'thcaped!' and his eyes went all big like soup plates. It was too much for Sam. She said, '*What?*'

'He'th 'thcaped!' said the Radish.

'Who has?'

'Wiffwid!'

'Where is he?' I said quickly.

Very solemnly, the Radish pointed at the floor. 'Thlithrin.'

'Quick! Catch him! Before he slithers away!'

Me and the Radish dived under the table. Giggling, we lurched about amongst the feet. Needless to say, *all* the animals came to join us. They couldn't understand what we were looking for!

No one could understand what we were looking for. When Wilfred had been rescued and put back in the Radish's pocket, Mum said, 'So what was all that about? Or shouldn't I ask?'

The Radish gave her this sweet little-boy

smile that he has, all impish and full of mischief.

'Wiffwid.' He patted his pocket. 'He'th aw wight now.'

'I'm relieved to hear it!'

'They're bonkers,' said Sam.

It's really not fair to have secrets, so later on I suggested to the Radish that we let Sam in on it.

'See, I can't tell her unless you agree. What d'you think? D'you think we should?'

'Yeth.' He nodded. 'Tell Tham. But nodda gwowd up!'

'Not the grown ups,' I agreed.

'Jud Tham.'

'Just Sam. I promise!'

I was a bit afraid that Sam might jeer, to pay us back for keeping things from her, but instead she took it dead seriously. Or at least pretended to!

'I knew it was a worm,' she said. 'I could see it, slithering about. Let's have a look at him!'

The Radish shot this little glance at me.

'It's OK,' I said. 'Sam can have a look.'

So next thing I know Sam's got Wilfred dangling from her fingers and she's waving him about, making him loop the loop and swing to and fro.

'Let's show him to Jack and Daisy!'

'Better not, they might eat him,' I said.

'They won't eat him! Come here, you two! I got something to show you.'

Jack and Daisy obligingly came and sniffed at Sam's finger, and Sam gave a little shriek and cried, 'Oh, you bad worm! Look, he's gumming at them with his gums!'

The Radish squealed and pummelled his cheeks, and Jack got silly and started barking, so then we decided that Wilfred had probably had enough excitement for one day and had better go back in the Radish's pocket.

'Otherwise,' said Sam, 'it'll all end in tears.'

'Yeth, 'coth wormth don't like dogth,' said the Radish.

'You didn't when you first came here,' said Sam. 'But you do now, don't you?'

'Do now,' agreed the Radish. 'Thpethly Jack an' Daithy. But Wiffwid'th mine. He'th my worm.'

'Oh dear!' said Sam later. 'The Radish is *so* funny.'

I said, 'Do you think we were like that when we were his age?'

'I suppose we must have been,' said Sam.

It made us feel very old!

The holidays came to an end and we had to go back to school. Larkhall Junior School is where me and Sam go. Mum said that the Radish was going to join us, only he was going to be in a different building, a little way down the road.

'I'll come with him tomorrow as it's his first day,' said Mum. 'But after that it would be an enormous help if you two girls could be responsible for him.'

Me and Sam didn't mind. We'd grown kind

of fond of the funny little Radish. It was a bit of a drag for Mum; she has enough to do. She helps Dad with his business, answering the telephone and making out invoices and paying all the bills. Dad has this ad in the *Yellow Pages*:

FOSTER FOR FAIR SERVICE

It comes under *Plumbers*, and people ring at all hours wanting Dad to go and fix their pipes or see to their washing machines.

So me and Sam said OK, we'd take the Radish to school in the morning and collect him again afterwards. No problem.

But that first day when we collected him, we knew straight off there was something wrong.

'How'd it go?' said Sam.

'Was it all right?' I said.

The Radish didn't say anything, he was too busy sucking his thumb.

'Hey, come on! Cheer up!' said Sam. She took his hand and tried to swing it. 'It can't be that gruesome!'

But it seemed that it was. When at last we got him to talk he whispered about 'big boyth' and being 'fwighted'.

'What about Wilfred?' I said. 'He wasn't frightened, was he?'

The Radish said that Wilfred had gone.

'*Gone?*'

'Gone where?' said Sam.

'Wun away.'

'He ran away?'

The Radish nodded.

'Why did he do that?'

''Coth the big boyth fwighted him.'

Sam and me looked at each other. We couldn't think what to say. I mean, if the Radish really believed that big boys had frightened his imaginary worm – well! There wasn't anything we could say.

And then I had a brainwave.

'Hey! Look!' I pounced. 'There he is! He must have come after you!'

And I scooped an imaginary worm off the

pavement and cupped it in my hands and showed it to the Radish, but his face just crumpled and the tears began to spurt.

That wasn't Wilfred! That was some other worm.

'Are you sure?' said Sam. 'It looks like Wilfred to me!'

But nothing would persuade the Radish. The big boys had frightened him, and he had gone.

That evening, me and Sam spoke to Mum about it.

'He's so unhappy, Mum! He's frightened! You can't make him go back!'

'Abi, he has to,' said Mum. 'He has to go to school. Everyone has to go to school.'

'But he's terrified,' said Sam.

'Look, I don't want to sound harsh,' said Mum, 'but he's got to learn how to stand on his own feet. If we mollycoddle him too much, he'll go on being terrified all his life long.'

Well! I always thought it was Mum who was

over-protective where the Radish was concerned. Now she was accusing me and Sam!

'Mum, you'll set him right back,' I said.

'Yeah! Just as he was getting on so well.'

'I think he ought to be allowed to get used to us before he has to start getting used to school.'

'He's already got used to us,' said Mum. 'And it didn't take him very long. It won't take him long to get used to school, either.'

Honestly, I never knew that Mum could be so hard. Me and Sam really hated having to take that poor little boy in to school next day. We stood at the school gates, the three of us, watching all the other kids as they rushed about the playground, and honestly! The noise they made! I'm sure we don't make that sort of racket in our playground.

The Radish had one hand clasped in mine. The other was up at his mouth and he was sucking his thumb like crazy. And he was shaking. Trembling all over from head to foot. How could we go away and leave him there?

'I can't do this,' said Sam.

I was about to say that I couldn't do it either, when this tiny little girl suddenly came trotting towards us across the playground. She had long blonde hair and big blue eyes and a gap in her teeth just like the Radish. She stopped, and beamed up at us.

'Who are you?' said Sam.

'I'm Thofie.'

'*Thofie?*'

'I think she means Sophie,' I said.

'I've come for Guth. Come along, Guth! You've got to come with me.' Gently, but very firmly, Sophie took possession of the Radish's hand. 'It'th all wight,' she said. 'I'll look after you.'

We watched as they toddled off together across the playground. They looked so cute!

Sophie with her long blonde hair and the Radish with his little red top knot, hand in hand.

'He'll be OK now,' said Sam. 'She won't let anyone frighten him.'

I didn't quite see how a little thing like Sophie was going to stand up to some of the great loutish boys in that playground, but Sam said she just bet she would.

'Just 'cos she's all pink and pretty, don't mean she can't fight. Anyone gives her any hassle, she'll soon sort 'em out!'

That afternoon when we picked the Radish up he was full of himself. He burbled all the way home about the things he had done in class and the games he had played in the playground, so I had to admit that Sam had probably been right. And I guess Mum had been right too, even though I'd thought her so hard-hearted.

'What about Wilfred?' I said. 'Has he come back yet?'

The Radish put his head on one side and thought about it.

'Ye-e-eth . . . he come back. But a big boy twod on him!'

'That was mean,' I said.

'Yeth, but then Thofie went *boff*!' The Radish made a fist and banged it triumphantly into the palm of his hand.

'She boffed him?'

'Yeth! She boffed him!'

'That showed him,' said Sam. 'And guess what? I've found you a replacement . . . look!' She whipped her hand from behind her back. 'A little baby mouse! Isn't he sweet? What shall we call him?'

'What colour ith he?'

'Can you see?'

We all peered at the imaginary mouse cupped in Sam's hand.

'He'th blue,' said the Radish.

'Blue?' said Sam. 'Are you sure?'

'Yeth. He'th blue.'

'So what shall we call him?'

'Call him Thofie.'

You can't argue with a six-year-old; they don't have the same powers of reasoning as we do. We agreed that the mouse was blue and that its name was Sophie. I mean, if it made him happy, what did it matter?

Quite soon the Radish stopped being six and became seven. Mum said he could have a birthday party and invite some of his friends from school, so me and Sam said we would help organise the games. On the day we blew up lots of balloons and tied them to the gatepost, so's everybody would know where the party was, and Dad cleared the front room to make a good big play space, while Mum and the Radish zoomed about the kitchen sticking veggie bangers on to sticks and opening bags of crisps and arranging mounds of chocolate pyramids and lemon curdles on a plate. Lemon curdles are something Mum made up. They are scrummy! Mum wouldn't let me and Sam into the kitchen as she said we were like gannets.

'You eat everything you can lay hands on!'

The party was a huge success. Loads of little kids came, including the Radish's girlfriend, Sophie. We tried teasing him about her, but he just said that she wasn't his girlfriend, 'She'th my *fwed*.' He meant friend but he couldn't say it, so we teased him about that as well, and started calling her Fred. The Radish didn't mind being teased these days. Sometimes he even pummelled us.

'*Thofie*,' he'd say. 'Her name'th *Thofie*.'

Me and Sam had tried to remember all the dotty little games that we'd liked to play when we were young. Musical Bumps and Pass the Parcel and Blind Man's Buff. We had to join in, of course; the kids insisted. It was all a bit beneath us, really, but it was worth it just to see the Radish's little radishy face all proud and beaming. And everyone had brought him presents! I don't think he'd ever had so many before. I'm not even sure that he'd had *any* before. He'd certainly never had a birthday party 'cos when the kids arrived and said 'Happy birthday, Gus!' and handed him the parcels they'd brought, he didn't know what to do with them. He took them all to Mum 'cos he thought they were for her. He couldn't believe it when Mum said they were his!

We'd all given him presents too, of course. Books and toys and jigsaw puzzles. Lots of *little* things, to make up for him having almost nothing of his own. Then on Monday morning, *three days* after his actual birthday, a card arrived from his mum. Inside was a five pound note and 'Love from Mum xxx'.

'Well, now! Isn't that lovely?' said Mum.

Very slowly, the Radish nodded. He didn't seem too certain.

'A card from your mum! And all that money, just to spend on yourself! What do you think you'll buy?'

'Dunno.' The Radish wriggled on his chair. 'Might not buy anyfing.'

'You want to save it? You can save it, if you like.'

But in the end, temptation overcame him. On the way back from school that afternoon we called in to the Minimart on the corner of the road and the Radish bought a yoyo. Yoyos were the thing to have just then. It was quite a special, posh sort of yoyo, bright red with silver swirls, and the Radish was dead proud of it. With what was left of his money he bought some sweets, which he insisted on giving to me and Sam. We were ever so touched!

'You don't have to do that,' said Sam.

'Want to,' said the Radish.

He wouldn't eat any of the sweets but he spent all the rest of the evening playing with his yoyo, and next day he took it to school with him. He wanted to show it to Sophie.

'Better not play with it in class,' I said. 'It gets the teachers really mad!'

That afternoon, at the end of school, a terrible mix-up happened. I don't know whether it was my fault or Sam's fault. See, Sam's in the netball team and sometimes, if we have netball last of all, Miss Russell keeps the team behind for just ten minutes to tell them about the next match or to have a bit of extra practice. I *knew* Miss Russell did this if we had netball last.

But Sam knew, 'cos I'd told her earlier, that I was going to stay behind and talk to Mrs Larkin about the end-of-term show. Sam's into sport and I'm into art, and I was going to help Mrs Larkin design the costumes. She'd asked me specially.

So we both of us *knew*; and what we should have done, one of us should have rushed down to the Juniors and picked up the Radish and brought him back with us.

Me probably. I just didn't think! I was so excited at being asked to help with the costumes.

Sam said she was just as much to blame, but she was only being loyal, because we're best friends.

The Juniors got out a few minutes earlier than we did, so usually the Radish just waited for us, inside the gates. I mean, me and Sam always turned up. It's just this one particular day we didn't; and instead of going back into school and telling a teacher, which is what he should have done, the Radish took it into his little radishy head to go wandering off by himself. He said afterwards that he thought we'd forgotten. Which I suppose, in a way, we had.

Me and Sam bumped into each other as we came out through the school gates.

'Help!' I said. 'Where's the Radish?'

'I haven't got him,' said Sam. 'I thought you were going to!'

'I thought you were!'

We stared at each other, aghast.

'Quick!' yelled Sam.

We tore helter-skelter down the road: the Radish wasn't there.

'Where is he?' I wailed.

A girl from our class, Lauren Babcock, who'd been hanging round with her best mate Alison Peach waiting to catch a glimpse of their hero, Lewis McEvoy, that's in Year 8 (they are just *pathetic*, those two) said that if we were looking for 'that little kid you pick up, he's gone without you'.

I felt my heart go plummeting, bang squish wallop, right down on top of my stomach. My stomach then plummeted too.

'Why didn't you stop him?' screeched Sam.

Lauren humped a shoulder. '*I* didn't know.'

That girl is such a dimbo!

'A little kid like that shouldn't be allowed to go off on his own,' grumbled Sam.

But we couldn't blame Lauren; it wasn't her fault.

'Mum's going to be absolutely furious!' I gasped, as I pounded after Sam.

It wasn't such a long way back to our house, but the Radish was such a sad weedy little creature. I think we both had these visions of him losing his way, or getting run over. Even *abducted*.

Sam ran like the wind, with me stumbling along behind. Sam is heaps taller than I am, and she has these really long legs that go galloping about like one of those huge great spiders the size of satellite dishes that race across the ceiling in the dead of night and terrify you. I, on the other hand, have quite *dumpy* little legs, more like the legs of a caterpillar than a spider. I find it almost impossible to keep up, but I did my very best. I was just so terrified that something awful might have happened to the Radish.

And then we rounded the corner, and we saw him. He was standing in the middle of the pavement and he was crying.

'Radish!'

We hurled ourselves at him.

'What's happened?'

'What's the matter?'

'Why didn't you wait?'

Between sobs and gulps the Radish told us that he'd thought we weren't coming.

'Tho I thtarted to walk home and – and thum big boyth . . . they thtole my yoyo!'

'Oh, *Radish!*'

'Which big boys?' said Sam.

The Radish said he didn't know which big boys. They were just big boys.

Me and Sam looked at each other. I knew we were both remembering the time he had told us that some big boys had trodden on Wilfred.

'Can you describe them?' said Sam. 'What did they look like?'

But the Radish sobbed and said again that they were just 'big boyth'.

'Which way did they go?'

'Downa woad.'

'That way?'

The Radish nodded.

'Ok,' said Sam. 'Let's go get 'em!'

We each took one of the Radish's hands and set off along the road. And we found those big boys! This time, the Radish had been telling the truth. They were a couple of great bullies that we'd seen before, hanging about on street corners. They were sitting on someone's garden wall and they were actually playing with the Radish's precious yoyo, honking and snorting with horrible coarse laughter.

I have to be honest: I was frightened! If Sam hadn't been there, I wouldn't have gone anywhere near them. I'd have gone running back home to get Mum. But Sam is really bold.

'Hey, you!'

She went marching up to them, all butch and bellicose, while I hung back with the Radish.

'What you want, squit face?'

'I want that yoyo,' said Sam.

'Go drown yourself! Ain't yours.'

'No, and it ain't yours, neither!' screeched Sam. 'You nicked it off my little brother!'

'What, him?' One of the boys jerked his head contemptuously in the Radish's direction. 'That little snotty-nosed nerd? Get lost!'

'You gimme that yoyo!' bawled Sam. 'Or I'll bash yer!'

'Oh yeah! You an' whose army?'

'Don't need no army! You just gimme it!'

I could feel the Radish all trembly, his hand hot and sticky as it clung to me. I felt a bit hot and sticky myself. I was just wondering if I should run for help when the other boy, not the one that Sam was yelling at, suddenly tossed the yoyo into the gutter.

'You wannit, you geddit!'

And then they both honked their horrible laughs as Sam grovelled on her hands and knees, just managing to rescue the yoyo before it could roll under the wheels of a passing car.

'You could have got hurt!' I hissed, as soon as we were safely round the corner and in sight of home. 'They could have gone for you!'

'Yeah, well, they didn't, did they?' said Sam. 'Here!' She handed the Radish back his yoyo. 'You just take care of it – and don't ever go wandering off without us again!'

'It was our fault,' I said. Mum was going to be *so* angry.

She would have been – if ever she had found out. She was dead worried when we finally showed up.

'Where have you been?' she cried.

I drew a deep breath. Sam said, 'We for—' And then, to our utter amazement, the Radish goes jumping in.

'I lotht my yoyo an' Tham an' Abi had to get it back f'me.'

'You lost it?' said Mum. 'How did you lose it?'

'Two big boyth thtole it off me,' said the Radish.

'Yeah, that's right,' said Sam. 'We had to chase 'em!'

'And it's taken you all this time?'

There was a pause. I swallowed. Sam gulped. I saw her Adam's apple pinging up and down. And then the Radish came rushing in again.

'We wan an' wan,' said the Radish. 'We wan for – ' he crimped his fists and began pummelling at his cheeks – 'we wan for thimply *mileth*!'

He could easily have told Mum that Sam and me hadn't picked him up when we should have done. But he didn't. He kept the secret. He was really one of us now!

6

Over the next few weeks, our little Radish really blossomed. We got ever so fond of him! He wasn't a drag any more. He played with the dogs and helped me rearrange the dolls' house furniture and nagged at me and Sam to play Snap, or Snakes & Ladders, or Happy Families. We didn't mind, not really. I mean, those sorts of games were dead childish but we reminded ourselves that he was only seven years old. It was like having a little brother: you have to keep them amused. And we really loved it when the Radish got excited and started making his funny little squeaking noises and pummelling his cheeks.

Snakes & Ladders was his all-time favourite. He squealed and pummelled like crazy whenever me or Sam had to go sliding down a snake! If *he* had to go down one, he'd let out his breath with a big 'Ouf!' and pound his fists together, all agitated. But if he got to go up a ladder, wow! You should have heard him crow. He'd give this great triumphant gurgle and rock backwards on his heels.

'It's only a game,' I told him, one time. 'You're not supposed to gloat!'

But I don't think the Radish had ever played games before. He took them really seriously; he just loved to win! Lots of times we let him, on purpose, though Mum said we shouldn't.

'It's not good for him! He's got to learn.'

But me and Sam couldn't resist it. It made him so happy! And we reckoned the Radish hadn't had very much happiness in his life. What did it matter if we let him win a few dotty little games of Snakes & Ladders?

'Helps build up his confidence,' said Sam.

This was a phrase she had heard Miss Davies use, though I'm quite sure Sam had never needed *her* confidence built up! She has more confidence than anyone I know. Some people say she's pushy, but they're just nerds like Lauren Babcock and Alison Peach. She's not pushy. She's just full of bubble and sparkle. She *fizzes*.

I couldn't ever see the Radish fizzing, but he was beginning to bubble and sparkle. In his own funny little gnome-like way. We'd discovered that he could be quite mischievous. One day, for instance, Dad came downstairs complaining that he'd lost his glasses.

There was this long pause while we all looked at him. Dad's glasses were on top of his head! He'd obviously pushed them up there and forgotten. That's my dad for you!

'Could you just run that past me again?' begged Mum. She cupped a hand to her ear. 'You've lost your glasses?'

'My glasses,' said Dad. 'My *glasses* . . . you know? Things you hook over your ears?'

Sam giggled, and so did I. Mum just rolled her eyes. And then, guess what? The Radish – little weedy Radish who wouldn't say boo to a flea – suddenly piped up.

'Ith there a w'ward?'

'A reward?' said Dad. 'For finding my glasses? Yes, why not? One pound for anyone that finds 'em!'

Mum threw up her hands. Sam and me were giggling fit to bust.

'I find 'em, I find 'em!' cried the Radish. He rushed over to Dad, scrambled on to the arm of a nearby chair and neatly plucked Dad's glasses off the top of his head. 'Now I gedda w'ward!'

Even Dad had to laugh.

'That'll teach me!' he said.

'Silly old man,' scolded Mum.

But I think secretly she and Dad were quite thrilled. It was the first time that the Radish had felt brave enough to play a bit of a joke on Dad. From that moment on, he and Dad were thick as thieves! They started going up the park together to play football, and one Saturday morning, when Sam was at her gym session and I was at my art class, Dad took the Radish out in the van on a plumbing job. The Radish came back all bursting with self-importance. He couldn't stop talking about it! It was 'Me an' Uncle' (Uncle was what he called Dad) 'me an' Uncle took the pipeth out, me an' Uncle dwilled a hole, me an' Uncle turned a water off!'

'We'll make a plumber out of you yet,' chuckled Dad.

Dad was ever so pleased the Radish had stopped being scared of him. It was the best victory yet!

Half term was coming up, and we were making all these plans for what we were going to do, like maybe visit the Chessington World of Adventure, like maybe go up to London, like maybe take the dogs down to the coast, when all of a sudden, wham bam, without any warning, right out of nowhere, the blow fell.

It was a really bitter sort of blow. It came in the shape of Miss Davies.

Well, I don't mean that Miss Davies herself was the blow 'cos as I've said before she is really quite nice when you get beneath the stony exterior. Miss Davies was more, like, the messenger. The person that delivered the blow.

The Radish was going back to his mum.

Of course, me and Sam weren't actually there when she broke the news. Only Mum and the Radish were there. And the Radish's own mum.

We knew that the Radish had seen his mum a couple of times, on Saturday mornings when me and Sam were at our classes, and it was quite true that Mum had told us, right at the beginning, he was only going to be with us a short while. We ought to have been prepared.

But we weren't. The news came as a terrible shock. We were devastated!

'It's good, isn't it?' gushed Mum. All bright and breezy, like we'd just won the lottery. 'It's what we've all been working towards!'

Mum might have been working towards it.

Me and Sam hadn't. It had taken us all this time to get that poor little pitiful Radish to trust us and now he was going to be snatched away!

'Told you this was what they did,' muttered Sam.

'But they can't!' I cried.

But of course they could.

Mum had to remind us that the Radish was only being fostered by us: not adopted.

'He has a real mum of his own, and it's time he went back to her.'

'Why?' That was Sam, all up-front and aggressive. She gets like that when she's upset. 'Why is it time he went back to her?'

'Because she's his mum!'

'So what?'

'Yes!' I said. 'So what?'

Mum didn't tell us off for being rude. She knew the news had come as a shock.

'Sam and Abi! We've already been through all this. You know perfectly well the point of fostering is to care for children until their real mums and dads are ready to look after them again.'

'She didn't look after him before,' said Sam.

'No, she didn't,' agreed Mum. 'Which was why he was taken into care. But now she's got herself a bit more together and she feels she can cope. So Gus is going to go back to her, because that is where he belongs.'

'She doesn't deserve to have him back!' Sam's face was one big scowl. 'She never took proper care of him! She let his step-dad wallop him! She let him hang labels round his neck! She's not fit to be a mum!'

Sam is very sensitive on the subject of mums.

'A person like that shouldn't be allowed to have children!'

I must say I agreed with her. But Mum pointed out that the Radish probably loved his mum in spite of her failings.

I said bitterly, 'It's like poor little dogs being

loyal to their owners even when they beat them.'

'Abi, Gus's mum never beat him.'

'No,' roared Sam, 'she just didn't look after him!'

'That was in the past,' said Mum. 'She won't let it happen again. She's learned her lesson. Gus is her little boy and she loves him.'

'Funny way of showing it!' snarled Sam.

Mum sighed.

'Sam, I know this is something you feel very strongly about. I know you both do. You've been so good with Gus, I can't praise you enough. I'm really proud of you both! But you've known all along he was only going to be here for a short time. He doesn't *belong* to us, Sam. We were just taking care of him. When you foster children you have to be prepared to let them go.'

'I'm being fostered and I'm not going!' declared Sam.

'No, you're not going.' Mum said it

soothingly. Sam was getting really worked up. 'You're staying with us for just as long as you want.'

'Forever!'

'Forever,' agreed Mum.

'So why can't the Radish?'

'Now, Sam, I've already explained! He's got a mum of his own and she's ready to have him back. And I'm sure that Gus will want to go back. Once he gets used to the idea.'

I frowned when Mum said that. Did that mean the Radish *didn't* want to go back? That he was being sent away against his will? If that were the case, then it was one of the wickedest things I ever heard!

'His mum deserves a second chance,' pleaded Dad a bit later on. 'Everybody deserves a second chance.'

'No, they don't!' shouted Sam. 'Not when it's their own fault!'

'His mum wasn't the one that ill-treated him, you know,' said Dad. 'That was her boyfriend.

113

She was probably just as terrified as poor little Gus.'

Sam glowered. 'She still ought to have done something!'

'Yes, she ought,' I said, feeling that Sam needed some support. 'Fancy letting him tie labels round his neck!'

'That was just *cruel*,' said Sam.

'Now listen you two.' Mum said it firmly. 'Just listen to me! This is difficult for all of us, including Gus. Please don't make it any harder than it already is.'

'But he doesn't want to go!' cried Sam. 'We're the ones he loves, not that woman!'

There was a silence. Mum bit her lip. Dad took his glasses off and pinched the bridge of his nose. I knew that really and truly they were every bit as cut up as me and Sam. They were just trying to be brave about it.

'Look,' said Mum. 'There's nothing we can do to change anything. The powers that be have made their decision: Gus is going back to his mum. That's all there is to it. It's up to us to help him.'

'Help him how?' I muttered.

'By not being so negative, for one thing! Try to be a little bit positive. Look on the bright side. Tell him how much his mum loves him, how much she's missed him, how much she wants him back!'

Sam looked rebellious. I knew what she was thinking. How *could* the Radish's mum love him? How *could* she? And let all those terrible things happen?

But I also knew, sadly, that Mum was right. If the Radish really did have to go back, we had to help him. I promised that I would do what I could.

'Thank you!' said Mum. 'I knew I could rely on you.'

I did my best, I really did. Sam couldn't face it. She went up to her room with Daisy and shut herself in. I stayed downstairs, with Mum and Dad and the Radish, and we all tried to assure him how wonderful it would be, to live with his real mum again. I said all the things Mum had told me to say.

'She loves you ever so much, Radish. Honestly! That's why she wants you back. She's really really missed you. And we'll really really miss you, too! So will Jack and Daisy. And Felix! But you can always come and see them. 'Cos we'll always be here.'

'Yes, and you'll only be living a short distance away,' urged Mum. 'You can come and visit whenever you want. And just think! You can even stay at the same school and be with all your friends.'

'With Sophie,' I said. '*Both* Sophies,' I added, and I gave him a little nudge and a wink and pretended to pull Sophie Mouse out of my pocket.

But the Radish didn't respond. He didn't respond at all. He hadn't said a word all the time we'd been talking to him. It was like he'd gone right back to the beginning again and all our hard work was for nothing.

'Maybe we could come and visit *you*,' I said cheerfully. 'Me and Sam! We could bring the dogs. We could all go up the park together. We could do that, couldn't we, Mum?'

'I'm sure you could,' said Mum.

'See? We can come and visit!'

'Don't you worry, fella.' Dad rumpled the Radish's little red top knot. 'It'll work out!'

All the rest of the evening the Radish sat on Dad's knee, sucking at his thumb like it was a lollipop. Sam had come down to join us, but she wasn't saying anything. She was cuddling Daisy.

Only a few weeks before, the Radish wouldn't have gone anywhere near Dad if he could help it. Now it was Dad he clung to. It seemed so sad! And there wasn't a thing that we could do. Miss Davies was the one who made the decisions, not us. Not even the Radish. The Radish was too young to make decisions; he was only seven years old. It's like being seven years old means you don't have any feelings. You don't have any *mind*. You just have to go wherever you're sent. Now he was being sent back to his mum, and it didn't matter one bit that it was making that poor little boy shake and tremble and suck his thumb.

Sometimes I think the world is a very cruel and unkind place. Mum kept saying it was 'all for the best'.

'It is, Abi! It really is. I know you don't think so at the moment, but he belongs with his mum, not with us. It will be all right. You'll see!'

That was what Mum *said*. But I had this feeling she didn't believe it any more than I did.

That night, for the first time in ages, the Radish wet the bed. He came creeping into my room, all damp and pathetic, and terrified once again in case he was made to wear the dreaded label. I did what I could to comfort him. I told him not to worry "cos it really doesn't matter', and I changed his pyjama bottoms for him and let him climb into bed with me and Jack, and we slept in a heap, all three of us, right round till morning.

We were still there, in our heap, when Mum came in.

'Oh, Abi!' she said; and just for a moment I almost thought she was going to burst into tears. I mean, I have never *seen* Mum burst into tears, she isn't a tearful sort of person; but that was what it looked like.

'I hate Miss Davies!' I told her later on that morning.

'Don't be silly,' said Mum. She said it rather wearily, as if this whole thing was just about wearing her out. 'She's only acting in the Radish's best interest.'

'Best interest!' I said. 'How does she—' And then I stopped. 'Mum!' I said. 'You called him the Radish!'

'Gus,' said Mum, hurriedly. 'I meant Gus.'

'No! He likes being called the Radish,' I said; and then suddenly I was starting to cry 'cos I just couldn't bear it, and Mum held out her arms and I ran into them and she said, 'Now, come on, Abi! You've got to be braver than this. We don't foster little people like Gus for our sakes; we do it for theirs. When the time comes to let go, we have to let go. You can't afford to become too involved.'

It was all very well Mum saying that, but sometimes you just can't help it.

7

On Friday afternoon we said goodbye to the Radish. Miss Davies came round, bringing this woman with her. This woman that was the Radish's mum.

Me and Sam just had a glimpse of her through an upstairs window. She was younger than Mum, and quite glam. Quite slim and prettyish. She had red hair like the Radish, and she was wearing this dead short skirt with a denim jacket. She didn't look like anyone's mum; more like a pop star or a model.

I tried as hard as I could to think good things about her, like for instance she really did love the Radish, like for instance she really had turned over a new leaf, like for instance she really was going to look after him properly. But it didn't matter how hard I tried, I just couldn't bring myself to believe any of it.

And I don't think Sam even tried.

'Look at her! Yeeurgh!' Sam made a being-sick noise.

'She is quite pretty,' I said.

'Pretty?' said Sam. 'You call that *pretty*?'

'Well . . . quite.'

'She's not pretty! She looks like some stupid freaked-out airhead!'

We watched as the stupid freaked-out airhead tottered up the path after Miss Davies, and then we couldn't see her any more 'cos they were under the porch. The reason she tottered was she was wearing these shoes with huge great heels about ten inches high.

'Hope she falls over and breaks her neck,' muttered Sam.

'Yes, then the Radish could stay with us!'

'I hate her. I *hate* her!' Sam aimed a kick at the wall. Her shoes left a dirty mark on the wallpaper but I didn't like to say anything. It didn't seem quite the right moment.

'What exactly *is* a freaked-out airhead?' I said.

'She is!' snapped Sam.

Me and Sam had already said our goodbyes. Mum had decided it would be best if we did it beforehand, so the Radish could go off all nice and quiet and not be upset. I think she was scared that I might blub or that Sam might make a scene. We probably would have done; it was bad enough just watching from the window. We saw this sad little procession going back down the path: Miss Davies, The Woman, and the poor little Radish, clutching at Mum's hand for all his worth. I mean, it was just too heartbreaking!

Sam couldn't take it. She flung herself on to the bed – the bed that had belonged to the Radish – and buried her face in Daisy's ruff.

'Tell me when it's over!'

I forced myself to keep watching. I saw Miss Davies hold open the car door and The Woman reach out and take the Radish's hand.

For one wild moment I was almost tempted to go and ring Childline and tell them that a poor little frightened boy was being abducted. Only I didn't have their number and in any case I knew there wasn't anything they could do. Nobody could do anything. Just helplessly stand and watch.

'Has he gone?' Sam's voice was muffled. She still had her face in Daisy's ruff.

'No. He's looking back. He doesn't want to leave us! Now his mum's—'

'Don't call her that! She's not his mum! Not a proper mum!'

'She counts as his mum.' And maybe she loved him. I had to hope so. He was such a funny little thing! How could anyone be cruel to him?

'What's happening now?'

I gulped. 'They're putting him in the car.'

'*Putting* him?'

'He's still looking back. He—'

'Don't!' Sam sprang up and pressed her

hands to her ears. 'Don't tell me! I don't want to know!'

'They're going,' I said. I could just make out the Radish's little white face, pitifully peering out of the car window. 'That's it! He's gone.'

All through the weekend I kept remembering the Radish's face, peering through the window. Mum said not to dwell on it, but it was like I had this video playing in my head, and it just played the same scene over and over again.

The following week was half term and we did all those things that we'd planned to do with the Radish. We took the dogs down to the coast and paddled in the sea and threw balls and collected interesting shells and long ropes of seaweed that you could pop, like bubble wrap. We went to the Chessington World of Adventure. We went up to town and visited the Toy Museum, which was brilliant as it has all these old dolls' houses, and I am really into dolls' houses. But all the time I kept thinking about the Radish, and how he would have loved it.

Every day I would say to Mum, 'I hope he's all right,' or 'I hope he's happy,' or 'I hope she's looking after him.' Sam didn't say anything. Whenever I mentioned the Radish's name she just went all tight-lipped and silent; either that, or left the room.

'Poor Sam! She's really taking it hard,' said Mum. 'We shan't be able to foster anyone else if this is what it's going to do to her.'

'It was just the Radish,' I pleaded. 'He was so little and sad.'

'But Abi, lots of children who need fostering are going to be little and sad.'

'Yes, but the Radish was special,' I said.

Monday after half term we went back to school. Sam and me had been hoping we could maybe go down to the Juniors and meet the Radish, same as we used to, but Mum said she'd rather we didn't.

'Not just yet; it would be too unsettling for

him. We'll have him to visit some time, but right now he needs to get used to being with his mum.'

'That's *rubbish!*' Sam said it very fiercely. She didn't say it to Mum, she said it to me, later on when we were alone. 'It's absolute *rubbish!* He'll think we've forgotten him!'

'But we couldn't see him anyway,' I said. 'He'd be gone by the time we get out of school.'

'Maybe. Maybe not.'

'Well, but he would! You know he always had to wait for us.'

'I bet he has to wait for that dimbo airhead, an' all! I bet she never turns up on time. Why don't we go and see?' urged Sam. 'We could easy bunk off school.'

'And get into a load of trouble!'

'So what?' Sam glared at me. 'If you're too chicken, I'll do it by myself!'

'But we promised Mum.'

'We never! She *told* us. We never promised!'

'Good as.'

'Well, I don't care! I want to see the Radish! I want to make sure he's all right.'

'Couldn't you just leave it for a *little* bit?' I begged. 'Then maybe we could both go.'

Sam grumbled, but in the end she agreed.

'I won't do it just yet. But I'm going to do it quite soon!'

'Just tell me first,' I said. 'Promise!'

Sam promised, and I knew she would keep her word. She kept muttering, 'I'm going to do it! I am! If we don't hear anything, I'm going to do it!'

After the first week, when we still hadn't heard (we couldn't ring up 'cos we didn't know the telephone number) Sam couldn't bear it any longer. She hissed at me 'I'm going to do it this afternoon!' And this time I couldn't stop her. We had music last thing with Miss Morgan. Miss Morgan is nice, but just the tiniest bit daffy.

'Tell her I've gone to the dentist,' said Sam.

'There'll be trouble,' I said.

'Think I care?'

'They'll find out.'

'Don't care! I'm still going.'

Sam went charging off and I obediently told Miss Morgan she'd gone to the dentist, which meant that now I would get into trouble too. Then Mum would hear about it and would say that I was 'under Sam's influence', which is something she quite often says owing to Sam having this rather bold personality and me (on the whole) being fairly quiet and retiring.

As soon as school was let out I went flying down the road to the Juniors. Sam was waiting outside the gates. She was looking worried.

'What happened?' I said. 'Did you see him? Is he all right?'

'I never saw him,' said Sam.

'You *missed* him?'

'He never came out.'

'Oh.' I fiddled with the catch on my school bag. 'P'raps he's . . . not well.

'Or something's happened to him.'

'What? What could happen to him?'

'Anything,' said Sam darkly. 'With that dimbo airhead!'

I really wished that we had the Radish's address so that we could have called round, but I knew it wasn't any use asking Miss Davies. She'd never let us have it. And we couldn't even tell her why we wanted it 'cos we weren't supposed to have tried seeing him.

'Do you think,' I said to Mum that evening, 'that the Radish could come round some time?'

'Some time,' agreed Mum.

'When? This weekend?'

'Maybe not quite so soon. We ought to give it a few more weeks.'

'But why?' I wailed.

'We don't want him coming round and being upset, do we?'

'You mean we don't want him coming round and not wanting to go back again!'

'Well . . . yes. Something like that,' said Mum.

'You mean he's not happy!'

'No; not necessarily. It's like when we adopted Jack. Do you remember? We brought him back from the rescue centre? And he was happy as could be! But if he'd been taken back to visit his original owner, it would have confused him. He wouldn't have known where he belonged – here, or there. It's the same with Gus. As soon as he feels settled and secure, I'm sure Miss Davies will say he can come round.'

'What's Miss Davies got to do with it? He's not being fostered any more!'

Mum said that Miss Davies was still keeping an eye on him. 'Just to make sure everything's all right.'

That was all that me and Sam wanted to do. Only no one would let us!

'We can't just leave it,' said Sam.

'But Mum said Miss D—'

'I want to find out for myself!' roared Sam. 'I'm going to bunk off school again and have another go.'

I was shocked. 'You can't do it twice!' We'd got away with it once. It would never work a second time.

'I'm going to!' said Sam.

I struggled for a moment. I think perhaps I am quite a wimpy sort of person compared to Sam.

'Maybe . . . I ought to do it,' I said.

'You?'

Sam knows I don't like getting into trouble.

'It'd be easier for me.' Nobody expects me to break the rules. 'I could bunk off PE. You could say it was my turn to go to the dentist.'

''kay.' Sam said it doubtfully. She didn't believe that I would really do it! But I wanted to know that the Radish was all right just as much as she did. All the same, I did feel a bit nervous when it came to the last lesson of the afternoon and I had to slip out of school without anyone seeing me.

'If he doesn't turn up,' hissed Sam, 'you gotta find someone an' ask!'

I had ages to kill before the Juniors were let out. I went into the sweetshop over the road and bought a candy bar and a copy of *Girls Weekly* and went to sit on a seat outside the Post Office until it was time. I was so anxious not to be late that I actually arrived at the school gates ten minutes early. I stood there, watching all the little kids come out and go running to their mums.

But not the Radish.

I knew I couldn't have missed him. There was just no way! I was starting to grow really desperate, wondering what to do and who to ask, when I suddenly caught sight of the Radish's little girlfriend, Sophie, coming across the playground.

'Hey! Sophie!' I cried.

She looked at me and beamed.

'Where's the Radish?' I said. 'I mean, Gus! Have you seen him?'

Sophie shook her blonde head. 'Guth ithn't here any more.'

'Not here? You mean—'

'He'th not here.'

A woman had come over; I recognised her as Sophie's mum.

'Hallo!' she said. 'You're . . . wait a minute, it'll come to me! Abi?'

'Yes,' I said. 'I wanted to see the R— I mean, Gus! But Sophie says he's not here.'

'That's right. She really misses him, don't you? He never came back after half term. We've been wondering where he'd got to. Mrs Baker doesn't seem to know.'

Mrs Baker was the Radish's class teacher. My heart sank. Sam was right! Something had happened!

I wanted to go rushing home and tell Mum right there and then, but I couldn't 'cos I had to wait for Sam. She was going to be at least another quarter of an hour. There was a netball match on Friday, so Miss Russell was bound to want a bit of extra practice or to do one of her talks.

I trailed back to my seat and sat there, miserably, thinking of all the terrible things that could have happened to the Radish. Suppose his step-dad had come back? The Radish was terrified of his step-dad. He was violent and horrible. He battered him and hung labels round his neck.

He could easily have slipped back without Miss Davies knowing. She didn't know everything. He could be there right now, terrorising the poor little defenceless Radish. He could have locked him in a cupboard. He could have chained him up. He could have—

I had to stop. I was scaring myself.

'I knew it!' cried Sam, when she finally arrived and I told her what Sophie's mum had said. 'I knew there was something wrong!'

'I don't know what to do!' I said. 'What should we do?'

'Tell Mum.'

'But she'll be mad at us!'

'What's that matter?' Sam turned on me

furiously. 'The Radish's *life* could be at stake!'

Just at first, Mum wasn't too pleased.

'Abi,' she said, 'I told you! I told both of you—'

'Yes, but Mum, something's happened to him! He never went back to school after half term and nobody knows where he is!'

'Not even his teacher,' said Sam.

Mum looked at us, frowning. 'How do you know?'

''Cos Sophie's mum told us!'

'Mum, we've got to do something!'

'I'll ring Miss Davies,' said Mum.

When she came back from speaking to Miss Davies, Mum was looking grave.

'Well, it seems you were right,' she said. 'The woman's done a bunk and taken Gus with her . . .'

8

'Why didn't she tell us?' I cried. I meant Miss Davies.

''Cos she felt too guilty!' snarled Sam.

'Actually it was because she didn't want to worry us,' said Mum. 'She's pretty certain the woman will surface sooner or later. For one thing, she's on Income Support. They'll be able to trace her.'

'Not if she's gone abroad,' said Sam. 'That's what they do, they snatch their kids and they go off abroad!'

'Miss Davies doesn't think she's done that. She thinks she's probably met up with some man and moved in with him.'

We stared at Mum, aghast.

'Not the *same* man?' I whispered. The one that had turned the poor little Radish into a quivering heap of jelly. 'Oh, Mum!

Not the same one!'

'I wouldn't think so,' said Mum. 'The woman knows perfectly well that if she took up with him again she'd lose Gus for good.'

'If he's still alive,' muttered Sam.

Mum didn't tell her not to be so silly and melodramatic. I knew that she was every bit as anxious as we were. She kept repeating that it wasn't Miss Davies's fault.

'She only did what she thought was best for Gus. We can all make mistakes. The woman was so plausible!'

'What's *plorzable*?' I said.

'It means that when she told people she'd turned over a new leaf, they believed her. *I* believed her!'

'The Radish didn't,' said Sam. She choked. 'He was so frightened! He didn't want to go! And she *made* him!'

That was almost the worst part. The memory of that poor little boy being torn away from Mum and forced to get into the car, even though he was making it as plain as could be that he didn't want to. And me and Sam had just stood there, watching!

The rest of that week was awful. We were all so sad and so worried, wondering where the poor little Radish had been taken and what was happening to him. Every time the telephone rang our hearts would leap 'cos we'd think it was Miss Davies telling us he'd been found. But it never was. One time it was Sophie's mum, wanting to know if we had any news. Mum told her about the Radish's mum doing a bunk, and she was really shocked. I could hear her voice coming over the phone:

'I sometimes wonder if these Social Services people know what they're doing!'

Mum defended Miss Davies, just like always. Mum thinks highly of Miss Davies, in spite of everything.

'They can't be expected to get it right all the time. Some of these people can be very deceiving.' And she told her about the Radish's mum being *plausible*.

'She even took me in. Until I actually met the woman I'd been a bit doubtful, to tell you the truth. I wasn't convinced it was such a good idea, sending the little chap back to her.'

Well! Mum had never admitted that to me and Sam.

'After I'd talked with her, I was right behind them. I felt they'd made the right decision. And of course, for all we know, she could be looking after him perfectly well.'

'Then why would she go running off?' hissed Sam.

And Sophie's mum echoed it over the telephone.

'If she meant so well, it's hard to think why she'd do a disappearing act. She was presumably supposed to keep in touch?'

'Yes.' Mum sighed. 'That was part of the agreement.'

'It rather makes you fear the worst.'

'I'm still keeping my fingers crossed,' said Mum. 'I haven't given up hope.'

But the days passed, and we still heard nothing, and it became harder and harder to believe that the Radish was safe and well. I tried not to be morbid or gloomy, but you can't always stop yourself from imagining things. I imagined lots of things that I would rather not have done. Sometimes they really frightened me.

And then on Friday, just as we'd got back from school, there was a strange eerie telephone call. It was me that answered the phone 'cos Sam was in the garden with the dogs and Mum had popped over the road to visit a neighbour. I clawed up the receiver and went, 'Yes?'

There was this long silence, and at first I thought whoever it was had dialled the wrong number and hung up, but then I heard what sounded like breathing, so I said, 'Hallo! Is anybody there?' And this tiny little thin trail of a voice whimpered, 'I'm cold! I'm tho cold!'

I went cold when I heard it. It was like icy fingers squeezing my heart.

'Who is that?' I said. 'Who is that speaking?'

There was a pause, and I thought I heard footsteps.

'Radish?' I said. 'Radish, is that you? Where are you? Is there anybody with you? Radish! It's Abi! Talk to me! Please!'

And then the line suddenly went dead and I just had this sinister feeling that somebody had come into the room and deliberately cut him off.

My immediate thought was that I had to tell Mum, so I grabbed up the telephone book and found the neighbour's telephone number and punched it out all wrong 'cos my hand was trembling so that I had to do it again, and this time I got through. Mum said, 'All right, don't panic! I'll come straight back.'

I was about to go rushing into the garden to tell Sam when the telephone rang again. I snatched up the received and cried, 'Radish?' But it wasn't. It was some stupid woman wanting the dentist. I shouted, 'You've got the wrong number!' and slammed the receiver back down. I didn't mean to be rude, but just suppose the Radish was still out there, still trying to ring us?

I raced into the garden and yelled, '*Sa-a-a-am!*'

'What?' bellowed Sam.

'I think I've just had the Radish on the phone!'

Mum must have flown back from the neighbour's. She arrived at the same time as Sam.

'The Radish?' shrieked Sam. 'Are you sure?'

'Tell me again what he said,' demanded Mum.

'He just said he was cold!'

'And you're really convinced that it was Gus?'

'Mum, it was! I know it was!'

'Did you get the feeling he was somewhere close? Or couldn't you tell?'

I hung my head. 'Couldn't tell.'

'Why didn't you get his number?' screeched Sam.

'I tried! I asked him! I asked him where he was, but . . . someone c-came and c-cut him off.'

'Ring 1471!' Sam clawed up the receiver and began punching out numbers.

'W-what's one f-four s-seven one?' I didn't even know what Sam was talking about.

'It tells you the number of the last caller,' said Mum. 'Well done, Sam! Quick thinking!'

My face fell. 'The last c-caller was a wrong number.'

'*What?*' Sam spun round, the telephone in her hand.

'It was a w-woman wanting the d-dentist.'

'You *idiot*! Why didn't you dial it immediately?'

'It all happened s-so quickly,' I stammered.

'So now we've still got no idea where he is!'

'Sam, don't be cross,' begged Mum. 'Abi wasn't to know.'

But I should have known! Sam had known. Why hadn't I?

'At least she hasn't taken him abroad,' said Mum. 'At least we know that!'

But we could have known a whole lot more. If only I hadn't been so useless! We could have known where the Radish was ringing from. The police could be racing to the rescue right now. If anything happened to that little boy, it would be all my fault!

Mum said that was nonsense. She told me, quite sharply, that I was not to blame myself. But how could I help it? Sam was cross as hornets. She sat in a simmering sulk all evening. I hated her being mad at me, but I knew that I deserved it. Sam would never have been so stupid. If she'd answered the phone, the Radish might have been safely back with us by now.

'Abi, I don't want you lying awake brooding,' said Mum, when it came to bedtime. 'You'd better drink some hot milk, it'll help you sleep.'

'Oh, Mum, no, please!' I begged. If there's one thing I loathe above all else, it's hot milk.

'It'll do you good,' said Mum. 'Whose turn is it to take the dogs in the garden? Is it yours, Sam? Right! Abi, off you go upstairs. I'll see to the milk.'

It was Sam who brought it up to me. She came into my room with both the dogs, and a tray containing two mugs of yucky hot skin-covered milk that made me feel sick just looking at it.

'Why two?' I said. 'I'm not going to drink two!'

'Yes, you are,' said Sam. 'It's your *punishment*.' And then she relented and said, 'One's for me.'

'But you don't like it any more than I do!'

'Mum said if you were drinking it, I'd got to keep you company. She said I'd been horrible to you. I'm sorry, Ab!' Sam threw herself on to my bed. Jack and Daisy hurled themselves after her. 'It wasn't your fault.'

'Yes, it was.' I said it glumly. 'Not knowing about—' I stopped. I'd forgotten it already! 'One-whatever-it-was.'

'1471. Tells you the number.'

'If only I'd known about it!' I wailed.

'You can't know everything.'

'You knew!'

'Yeah. Well.' Sam humped a shoulder. 'Just one of those things, innit?'

'But the Radish could have been rescued!'

'Don't worry. He's bound to ring again.'

I knew she was only saying it to try and make me feel better, but I gave her a bit of a smile and pretended to believe her.

'Next time I'll be ready for it. I'll ring that number, like you said. Look!' I seized a pen and scrawled it, very big, on the back of my hand. '1471. Now I can't forget!'

'Better not wash your hand,' said Sam.

'I won't!' I vowed. 'Not until the Radish is back.'

We drank our foul hot milk (we gave the skin to the dogs) and Sam went off to her room. Me and Jack snuggled down under the duvet. I didn't think that I would ever be able to get to sleep. My head was full of dreadful images, like the poor little Radish being terrorised, being battered and bruised, being kept locked up, being *cold*.

'I'm cold! I'm tho cold!'

His voice still rang pathetically in my ears. Mum had told us how the Radish's mum had been in the habit of going off and leaving him on his own, locked into a room, for hours on end. Sometimes all night long. Once she had gone off for a whole weekend and left him, which was when the neighbours had become suspicious and reported her.

I just couldn't bear the thought of the Radish cold and scared and hungry, all by himself in a locked room. And in spite of what Sam had said, I didn't really believe that he would ring us again. Next time they would make sure he couldn't get at the telephone.

I tossed and turned for what seemed like ages but maybe there is something in Mum's hot milk theory after all, or maybe I was just worn out with guilt and misery, 'cos to my surprise I actually managed to fall asleep. I mean, I didn't *say* to myself, 'Oh, here I am falling asleep.' I mean, you never do. It's not the way it happens. The way it happens is one minute you're awake, the next minute you're not. But I must have fallen asleep 'cos the next thing I know Jack's come shooting up the bed as if there's a bug-eyed monster after him and I'm going, 'What, what? What's the matter?'

I tried to stuff him back again under the duvet, but he wouldn't go. He just sat there, bolt upright, with his ears all of a-quiver, then quite suddenly he dives off the bed and runs to the door, where he begins this frantic scratching.

'Jack, stop it!' I begged.

I really hate having to go downstairs and let him out in the middle of the night. It's dark and creepy and I always imagine that things are waiting to pounce at me from the shadows. I suppose I'm a bit of a coward, to tell you the truth.

'Jack! *Please*,' I said. 'Be a good boy! Come back to bed!'

But he wouldn't. He can be really stubborn. He put his nose into the air and began that weird singing that dogs do. A sort of cross between a howl and a hoot. It's quite scary. Especially in the middle of the night!

'What is it?' I whispered; but he just scrabbled even more frenziedly at the bottom of the door.

In the end I had to get up and put my dressing gown on and take him downstairs. I let him out of the back door and he went tearing off into the darkness, barking fit to bust. It was the shrill yappy bark he does when he's found something and wants you to go and look. But I wasn't going. No way! I opened the door about half a centimetre and hissed, 'Jack! Shut up!' The neighbours would complain, and then Mum would get mad.

'*Jack!*' I sort of bellowed it, softly. '*Be quiet!*'

And then I heard footsteps, and Dad appeared in the kitchen.

'Abi? What's going on? Why is that dog making all that racket?'

'I don't know.' I stood helplessly on one leg, like a stork. 'I think he's found something.'

'Well, he'd just better stop it or we'll have the whole neighbourhood up in arms.'

Dad went charging out into the garden, with me following. I felt a bit braver with Dad there! Jack was at the back gate, tearing at the bottom of it with his claws.

'Go back and get the torch,' said Dad.

I tore back to the kitchen, grabbed the torch from the kitchen drawer and went racing out again. Jack had now stopped barking and was snuffling excitedly.

'Grab him,' said Dad.

I bundled him into my arms. Dad eased the gate back just a crack and shone the torch through.

'What the—'

'What is it, what is it?' I quavered.

We have a covered pathway running all up one side of the house and I have always been scared of what might linger and lurk there in the dark.

'Dad! Don't open it!' I pleaded.

But Dad had already done so. Jack sprang out of my arms and went bounding forward.

'Get your mum!' cried Dad.

'W-why?' I said. 'W-what is it?'

'Get your mum, quick! It's Gus!'

He was huddled there, cold and wet and sobbing. Dad carried him ever so gently indoors and Mum came down, and then Sam, and we all kissed and cuddled him and Mum made him a warm drink while Dad took his wet clothes off and wrapped him up in a blanket. The dogs were going crazy, trying to lick him, and even Felix, who'd been sleeping on top of the fridge, opened an eye and regally wandered down to have a look.

We tried to piece together what had happened. The Radish sat on Dad's lap and between sobs and hiccups did his best to tell us. He said his mum had taken him to live 'in another houth' and that there was 'a man' there and his mum and the man had gone out and left him and he had been scared.

He had also been cold, 'cos there wasn't any heating.

'Is that when you telephoned?' I said.

'Yeth.' The Radish nodded. He had climbed on to the table and tried to reach the telephone, but he hadn't been able to, so then he'd put a chair on the table and climbed on to the chair. They had obviously put the telephone really high up so the Radish couldn't get at it. But he'd managed to! He had rung our number and I had answered, but he had only had time to tell me that he was cold before his mum and the man had come back and the man had snatched the telephone away from him and his mum had been cross and slapped him.

'Then what happened?' said Sam.

The Radish said that his mum and the man had started to fight (which must have absolutely terrified him. He hates it when people get angry). The Radish had hidden in a corner while they shouted and yelled, until in the end the man had gone storming out and his mum had gone racing after him. Only in her hurry she had *forgotten to lock the door*. So after a bit the brave Radish had crept out from his corner and sneaked into the hall, tiptoed down the stairs, out through the front door and found his way home. He really was a *clever* little Radish!

We discovered later that they hadn't been

living all that far away. Miss Davies said they had been planning to go to Scotland. If that had happened, the Radish might never have come back to us! He could never have found his way back from Scotland. As it was, he had been crying through the streets all night long, trying to remember where our road was. He knew that it was near a park, and he knew where the park was, but after that he'd got hopelessly lost and didn't know which way to go.

There are five roads that lead to the park, and the poor little Radish had trudged down every single one of them until he found us! And then he had crept round the side of the house and huddled into the corner of the wall and the back gate to wait till it was light.

'Oh, Radish!' I cried, when he managed to tell us about it next morning. 'Why didn't you ring the bell?'

Guess what he said? He didn't want to wake us up! That is so like the Radish. He is such a meek little boy. He never wants to upset people or be a nuisance. I just don't know how anyone could be unkind to a little boy like that.

Anyway. He was back! And this time it was for keeps. I mean *really* for keeps. His mum told Miss Davies that he could be put up for adoption and Miss Davis has said there isn't any reason why we shouldn't be the ones to adopt him. It's what we want, more than anything, and it's what the Radish wants, too. So maybe one day soon he won't be Gus Radice any more, he'll be Gus Foster!

Except that he'll always be the Radish to us.